FINDING
LOVE

Kale Bradley

CONTENTS

CHAPTER 1

"I'm sorry, Baby. Just come home, I miss you so much." Vonne said.

"I miss you too, baby. I've been dreaming about this day. Let daddy kiss those beautiful lips. " Briell said. He puckered his lips and stuck out his tongue with his eyes squeezed shut.

"Eww Mama, Briell is kissing an invisible person, " Jasmine screamed out to their mom who was downstairs. At the sound of her squeal, Briell awoke from his sleep.

"Jassy, what are you doing in my room?" He asked groggily.

"No, the question is who were you kissing in your sleep? Was it Vonne?"

Briell shot Jassy a look that caused her to burst into laughter. She began puckering her lips and sticking her tongue out, just as he did a few moments ago. Annoyed, Briell threw a pillow at her, knocking her small body down.

"I'm going to tell mama." She squealed as she ran downstairs.

Briell laid back down and stared at the ceiling. "Damn, I actually thought that dream was real."

A few seconds passed before his mom stormed into his room, "JaBriell Rashad Gibson, get your ass up, why are you throwing pillows at your sister?"

Briell sat up to see his mom with her hands on her hip and Jasmine behind her, puckering her lips and shaking her head and body from left to right, teasing him.

"I'm up, Ma. What's up?" Briell said.

"What's up? I cooked for y'all, and the food is getting cold. You know how I hate that, come and eat. Also don't take your anger out on Jassy because you still in your feelings about that damn girl. Get your shit together, and clean this room up, damn." His mom finished before walking out the doorway. Jassy still stood in the doorway laughing at him and doing a little dance to taunt him. He smiled at her and raised a fist up.

"I'm going to get you back." He murmured so his mother couldn't hear him.

"Jassy get your butt down here and eat." Their mother called out loudly. She stopped teasing her brother instantly and ran down the stairs.

Briell finally climbed out of bed and checked his phone. He had a couple texts from his homeboys and a missed call from his job, along with one new voicemail. He figured it was from his supervisor. *"I wonder why he didn't text me?"* He thought to himself while throwing on a pair of basketball shorts and a t-shirt. Briell wasn't moving fast enough as his mother began to call out to him again

"JaBriell." She yelled from downstairs.

"I'm coming now, Ma." He answered leaving his room swiftly.

JaBriell was twenty-five years old. His mother Stephanie was only seventeen when she had him. His mother and father were high school sweethearts. Jamaal Gibson was the star running back for Hillsborough High School. Stephanie was a beautiful cheerleader. They met at Hillsborough High. Before their high school graduation JaBriell was born. Together they decided to go to USF. Jamaal was offered a scholarship at FSU, FAMU, and USF. He chose USF so he could be with JaBriell and Stephanie.

Jamaal was a country boy who was raised in Thonotassasa. He was supposed to go to Armwood High School, but his cousin lived on the east side and went to Hillsborough, so he used his aunt's address to attend Hillsborough High also. Jamaal's parents had been together for over thirty years. He was raised to be a family man, one that took care of his family. When Stephanie got pregnant and had JaBriell, he made a vow to never leave her or the baby.

Stephanie on the other hand was raised in the hood. She was a go yam, straight from Ponce de Leon projects. She was one of the finest chicks in the whole neighborhood. All the guys wanted her and her crew. Stephanie was a light brown complexion, shapely body, long hair and light brown eyes. She was hood, but she was smart. She was an honor student since junior high. Her and Jamaal were opposites, but once they met each other, they were stuck like glue. Stephanie would fight other girls for flirting with him. Jamaal loved her gangster ways. She would even straighten him out if he got her wrong.

While they were in college, Jamaal's family watched JaBriell. He grew up away from the hood. Once Stephanie and Jamaal graduated from USF, they both obtained good careers. Jamaal got hurt during his senior year at USF, so he decided to continue his degree in pharmacology. He became a pharmacist at St. Joseph's Hospital. Stephanie loved children. Once she had JaBriell, she would always have all her friends' babies or cousins' babies over for parties and sleepovers. Stephanie and Jamaal saved enough money and opened a daycare center. Jamaal was always too busy to help her run it, so Stephanie hired her cousin Lela and best friend Rosemary to help her run the daycare.

When JaBriell was five years old, they moved into a nice home in Town and Country. Stephanie and Jamaal were young and successful, their money was straight, their daycare center was booming, they had officially made it. Jamaal wanted a little girl, but Stephanie didn't want to have any more kids. Jabriel grew up wanting for nothing. He always had the latest clothes and shoes. He even had a car at fifteen years old. His pops taught him how to drive when he got his learner's permit. Even though JaBriell wanted for nothing, his mom was strict on him, and Jamaal taught him family values.

He attended church, and he didn't hang out with the wrong crowd, his grades were good, and the girls loved him. Stephanie thought it was cute when he was younger how little girls would be all over him, but when he became a teenager, he became more handsome, his build was forming, and his smile could light up a room. She became a hater and felt as if those fast-ass little girls would turn him out or corrupt him. Dating was off limits until he was sixteen.

One afternoon JaBriell and his pops went out to drop some things off at Stephanie's mom's house, on the east side, off 22nd street. Projects once stood in the place of the newly built homes in the area. Stephanie's mom acquired one of those newly built homes. JaBriell's father allowed him to rive his brand-new Benz on the way to his grandmother's house. The moment they arrived, JaBriell hugged his grandmother tightly.

"Boy, you're getting bigger and more handsome by the day." She smiled. "You have to start coming to see your grandmother more, especially since it's summer. I need my grass cut from time to time."

"Yes, ma'am. I'll come by whenever you need me. My dad just bought me a car, but I have to get my license before I can drive without him. I'm taking my test next week. He's been letting me drive him around with him so I can practice. I'm getting the hang of it." He informed her.

"Ok, baby. I'll be waiting for you." She then turned her attention to Jamaal, "How're you doing, son? Thanks for dropping this insurance policy paperwork off. I don't know why your wife insists on filling everything out for me. I told her I could have done it."

Jamaal smiled and said, "You know how she is, Momma. I'm glad she completed it paperwork, however. Those insurance companies are slick, and we need everything to be right for your policy."

"Well, Thank you all for that." She said taking the policy into her hands, "JaBriell, are you hungry? I made some okra, beans, yellow rice and fried chicken." She announced.

"I'll take some yellow rice and chicken, but what's okra?" JaBriell asked with a serious face. Big momma and his dad both burst into laughter.

"My Lord, Jamaal, what are you and Stephanie feeding this boy? He can't survive off McDonald's. Come on, JaBriell, let me make you a plate, and I'll make your momma a to-go plate also."

When summer began, JaBriell kept his word and visited his grandma to help her out around the house and in the yard. One weekend, he was cutting the grass. He pulled his shirt off and began to drink a glass of Kool-Aid while taking a short break. He noticed a group of girls looking at him from across the street. He waved, and one of the girls walked towards him. He suddenly became nervous. He tried to keep his cool as she approached him.

"Who are you?" she asked bluntly.

"I'm JaBriell. What's your name?" he returned.

"I'm Yvonne, but everybody calls me Vonne." She was talking, but he wasn't listening. His mind was focused on her body that was clothed in the short shorts hugging her tight frame. Her breasts stuck out of the tight T-shirt she wore, also. Her hips and butt were huge. Her body was glistening from the heat. Her toes were freshly done as he admired her feet in those sandals. Her hair extended down her back. She was honestly the prettiest girl he had ever seen.

She snapped her finger in JaBriell's face snapping him out of his trance. "Hello?"

"Huh, what did you say?" he asked quickly.

"What school do you go to?" she asked with a bit more attitude.

"Oh, I go to Jefferson High." JaBriell answered.

"That's what's up, I go to Gaither High." Vonne returned.

"Why do you go there? It's super far." Briell asked scratching his head.

"I know, right, But it's in our district. It's crazy. If you stay on this block you go to Gaither, but around the corner they go to Hillsborough." Vonne expressed. "Who lives here?"

"My grandma, I come over to help her out sometimes." He answered.

"Oh, that's what's up. Put my number in your phone and hit me up when you're over here. I'll pull up on you." Vonne smiled. JaBriell pulled out his phone, and happily exchanged numbers with her.

"I see you have the new iPhone. I settled for a Samsung, but it do, what is do." Vonne shrugged coyly. JaBriell loved her lingo. The people he hung out with didn't speak like that. They didn't say things like pull up on you, or it do what it do. They spoke much more proper. He wasn't even sure what pull up on you meant, but he played it off well. From that day forward him and Vonne have been boyfriend and girlfriend.

JaBriell and Vonne were like his parents. JaBriell wasn't hood at all, but Vonne was. Vonne was the first and only person he had sex with. She was the only girl he had a relationship with. His parents were unaware he was in a relationship for some time. When he turned seventeen, his little sister was born, and their focus was diverted to her. By the time his mother found out about his relationship it was much too late, JaBriell was in love, and there was nothing she or anyone else could do about it.

Fast forward to seven years later, JaBriell and Vonne broke up. He moved out of their apartment and returned home with his parents and his annoying little sister.

CHAPTER 2

J aBriell sat at the table picking over his plate, he had been struggling to regain his appetite for some time. Jassy on the other hand had no issue eating, she was already tearing into her third piece of bacon.

"Son, you have to eat. I know everything is still fresh with you and Vonne, but you have to snap back to reality."

"Snap back, baby," Jassy said snapping her fingers in front of his face.

"Are you at least going back to work, Monday? I'm pretty sure they need you." Stephanie asked.

JaBriell followed in his mom's entrepreneurial footsteps. He opened a sandwich shop in Town and Country. They were known for making the best Cuban sandwiches in town. When him and Vonne broke up, he decided to take some time off. He allowed the manager of the shop to run things until he was mentally ready to return.

"I'm trying, Momma. I just don't know what happened. I thought we were going to get married." JaBriell revealed solemnly.

"Son, every high school relationship doesn't last for the long haul. Sometimes people want different things, and sometimes people grow apart." Stephanie advised. JaBriell stared into space, while Jassy snatched a piece of bacon off his plate. He caught her and began tickling her. Jassy laughed and screamed.

"Y'all better stop playing at my table. Jassy, hurry up and eat so we can get to the mall. And Briell, you need to clean your room up and get some life back in into you. You're too young to be acting like this. Shit, boy, you got your own business, you look good, no kids, you just don't know you're every woman's dream."

"Mommy, I'm done." Jassy said with a mouthful of food.

"Well, go and get ready. I put some clothes out for you. And wash your face, please." Stephanie ordered her.

"Ok, mommy." Jassy agreed as she got up from the table and punched JaBriell in the back. He took off running behind her. When he caught her, he picked her up in the air and carried her upstairs. Jassy laughed and screamed all the way to her room.

Within the next hour, Stephanie grabbed her *Michael Kors* purse in prepapration to leave. Before leaving the house, she stopped by Briell's room once again.

"Your father said you two can meet and grab a bite to eat, once he gets off work today. He's off at three, I'll see you later, baby."

"Bye, Briell. Don't cry, ok?" Jassy remarked.

"Girl, come on and leave your brother alone."

JaBriell was finally home alone. He sent a text to his boys, Thadd and Squirt. They were friends since middle school. They all grew up in Wesley Chapel. Thadd was a science teacher and Squirt was still trying to figure life out. He was basically living off his parents' money. Neither of them was busy at the time, so he Facetimed them.

"How're you holding up, bro?"

"He better have his head held high. There's an old saying, *there's plenty of fish in the sea*. All you have to do is go fishing." Squirt advised.

"Come on, Squirt, he doesn't need to get involved with someone else, right away. He needs to get himself straight, first." Thadd reasoned.

"There you go, always trying to be nice and subtle about situations. Fuck being nice and subtle, what you need is a chick to take your mind off Vonne. Best believe she's doing her thing, without you. I saw her on Instagram with her rachet-ass friends. You're sick, and she's doing well." Squirt compared.

"Listen, Briell, take as much time as you need. Do what's best for you." Thadd tried to soothe his friend.

"Yeah, get you some booty, some new booty." Squirt added.

"I need to get out of this house. I need to kick it with my boys today. Let's meet up." Briell suggested.

"Yeah, that's cool. I'm not doing anything, anyway."

"Yeah, as always." Thadd returned.

"Whatever, Science Man. Yo, Briell, where do you want meet at?" Squirt ignored the comment from Thadd.

"Let's meet up in an hour at Joe's Barbeque off Water Street." Briell answered quickly.

"Bet." Squirt and Thadd said in unison. They hung up, and within an hour they were all are ordering food at Joe's. Once they finished ordering, Squirt pulled out his phone and scrolled over to JaBriell's Facebook page.

"Bro, why haven't you changed your relationship status?" He asked noticing that Jabriell's status still stated that he was in a relationship. He then went over to Vonne's page and saw that her status read single single. He slowly turned his phone around and showed Briell what he was talking about.

"She's claiming that she's single. You need to change your status. You look like a sucker for real." Squirt urged Briell.

"I hate to agree with Squirt, but he's right." Thadd said.

"Well, hallelujah." Squirt chuckled a little. Briell picked up his phone up and changed his relationship status to single. He did the same to his Instagram page once he noticed Vonne took all of their pictures down and replaced them with new pics and vines of her and her girls hanging out partying. He clicked on one of the vines and saw her and Constance in the club. Constance was screaming, "*My girl single.*" The two of them were dancing, and Constance slapped Vonne's butt, then some guys gathered around them and started dancing on them.

When the vine came to an end, Squirt commented immediately, "Don't sweat it, bro. My homie Deek is having a party tonight, and we're going. It's time you got your mojo back."

"Man, I've never been with any girl besides Vonne. I don't even know what to say to a chick."

"Wait, when you say you've never been with another girl, do you mean relationship-wise or sexually?" Thadd asked quickly.

"Both." Briell shook his head, a bit ashamed of what he had just admitted.

"My bad, bro. I just can't believe Vonne is the only girl you've been with." Squirt said as he laughed aloud as the waitress sat their plates before them.

"Let's pray before we eat." Squirt suggested.

Thadd and Briell look at each other confused, as Squirt began to pray, "Lord, please bless this food we are about to eat. Lord, please bless Briell with a girl with a phat booty. Lord, allow him to embrace the booty."

"Well." Thadd chimed in.

"Lord, give him the strength to touch and caress the booty." Squirt continued.

"Yes, Lord." Briell screamed out in agreeance.

"Lord, we ask all these things in your name. Amen." Squirt finished. They began laughing and giving each other dap and high fives.

"It's good to see you smiling again." Thadd said before digging into his food.

"We're turning all the way up tonight." Squirt cheered enthusiastically. He then snapped a few pictures of them eating, along with a picture with the waitress and posted them.

CHAPTER 3

Briell, Thadd, and Squirt parked on Deek's block, observing how many cars were lined up.

"Y'all ready?" Squirt asked looking at each of them.

"Damn, Deek brought the city out." Thadd said looking around. Just as he spoke three girls walked past Squirt's Lexus towards the house party. They all had on skimpy dresses showing off all their curves and angles.

"Wow this is crazy. Who would have known Deek would become this popular?" Briell shook his head in disbelief. Each of them had known Deek since middle school. Deek was one of the coolest white boys in Tampa. His Mom and Pop were rich. Deek was attracted to the urban culture. He always had black friends and girlfriends. They all grew up in Wesley Chapel together. Once they graduated from high school, Deek's popularity skyrocketed. His parents threw him a huge party and Drake performed. Since that day he's been both Instagram and locally famous. All the high school and college students flock to his parties.

His parties became so out of control that the Wesley Chapel community fined his parents. After receiving so many fines, the association tried to kick them out of the community. His parents bought him a house in the Timberlake subdivision. Squirt and Deck were cool. Squirt had all access to Deek's parties, whether it was at a club or house. Briell, Thadd, and Squirt were from Town and Country, so everyone knew them also. There were a few people hanging outside the house as they walked up. They greeted them as they walked into the house. The moment Squirt opened the door, the whole atmosphere changed. The DJ was spinning Future's new song as strobe lights flickered and hundreds of people partied.

"Yo, Deek, what's up?" Squirt greeted as soon as he spotted Deek.

"My Brodie, Squirt. What's happening? Glad you could make it." They dapped each other up and then shared a man hug.

"Yo, I know you remember my dawgs Thadd and Briell." Squirt said stepping to the side.

"Yeah, I remember them. We all had those dumb-ass swimming lessons at the community pool when we were kids." Deek laughed. The guys joined him in a laugh and then offered him dap also.

"Well, boys, we aren't kids any more, this is my community, drink whatever you want, smoke whatever you want, and have any girl you want. Everything is on me." Deek welcomed.

"Alright, my G, I'm out. Have a good time. I have to tend to some guests." He pointed to a group of girls in bikinis. They want me to join them in the jacuzzi." He revealed before walking away.

"It's time to take shots." Deek yelled with a bottle of Ciroc in the air. The crowd went wild as a few girls came out carrying trays filled with shot glasses.

"It's turn up time." Squirt yelled.

The three of them took a shot and chased it with another. Feeling relaxed they began to dance and have a good time. Thadd was happy to see his best friend laughing and having a good time. Squirt took pictures of them and recorded a few vines. An hour passed and everyone was having the time of their lives. Squirt walked up to the DJ booth and said something to him. Suddenly, the music stopped. Squirt took the mic into his hands and the house became quiet.

"I want to send a shout out to my main man Deek for throwing this live-ass party. Show Deek some love." Squirt said with all eyes on him. Deek stood up on the couch as everyone around him cheered.

"I want everyone to take a shot for my dawg, one of T.C.'s finest, JaBriell. Him and his girlfriend broke up, and he's single, now. Everyone that's single take a shot for Briell and let's turn up in here." He finished. The DJ began playing Lil Kee's *Bust It Open.* The girls started dropping it low, as everyone took shots. The party became even liver than it was a few short moments earlier. Five girls began dancing on Briell. At first, he was embarrassed that his friend put his business out there, but after the girls surrounded him, he felt better. The three of them continued to drink and enjoy themselves. Thadd had a bit too much to drink and found himself sick. Squirt recorded Thadd throwing up in the trash can.

Squirt wanted to capture all the moments; he began recording Briell who was getting a lap dance. Everyone around him cheered him and the girl on. Thadd noticed Squirt recording him and began chasing

Squirt around for three minutes until he ran out of air. The alcohol had a major effect on Thadd because he was in perfect shape, he worked out constantly. Thadd bent over on the couch, trying to catch his breath.

"Erase the recording." Thadd demanded as Squirt came walking up beside him.

"What recording?" Squirt asked with a clueless expression.

"The one of me throwing up, asshole." Thadd said.

"Oh, I thought you wanted the one I'm recording right now erased." Squirt laughed. Thadd tried to grab Squirt's phone, but his reaction was too slow. Squirt laughed and moved out the way each time.

"I can't afford to have one of my students see me like this, Squirt." Thadd admitted holding his stomach. Quickly, he put his hand over his mouth and ran back into the kitchen and threw up, again. A group of people were in the kitchen while he threw up, they all began to cheer.

Squirt continued to record Thadd, whose head was in the trash can. Squirt walked closer flipped the camera around, while putting his head closer to Thadd.

"I love this guy." He spoke into the camera that was now in selfie mode.

"Squirt, you're a dick." Thadd said finally mustering the strength to stand up straight.

"I love you, man." Squirt said with his arm around Thadd's shoulder. Thadd shook his head from left to right, while smiling. He puts his arm around Squirt who helped him up over to a chair.

"You're still an asshole." Thadd said in a low tone as Squirt finally stopped recording him.

"Try to sober up, big guy. I'm going to find Briell." Squirt patted Thadd's shoulder before walking away to find Briell.

Thadd closed his eyes to trying to sober up, while two sexy girls took a seat beside him. One sat on his left side, and the other one on his right side. A third girl stood in front of them recording as the two girls made silly faces. They were making fun of Thadd, who was now sound asleep. One girl lifted her shirt and put her breast on Thadd's mouth. She made sexy faces while her other friend took pictures of it. The other girl straddled him and turned her head around to the camera, making sexy faces as if she was riding Thadd. She was wearing a skirt, which aroused Thadd. The girl felt the stiffness on her love box. Immediately, she jumped off Thadd's lap and showed her friends the erection poking through his jogger-style pants.

The girls were amazed at the size, they each took turns taking pictures. One girl wrapped her hand around it as she smiled at the camera. The other girl put her head in his lap as if she was about to give him a blow job. Lastly, two of the girls got back on the couch, one on each side of him, and stuck their tongues out by his crotch as Squirt and Briell walked up beside them.

"What the hell are y'all doing?" Squirt questioned observing the scene. The girls laughed and then walked away. Squirt nudged Thadd, in effort to wake him up and noticed he had a hard on.

"Why is his dick hard?" Briell questioned. Thadd slowly woke up from his sleep.

"Come on, buddy. We have to get you out of here." Squirt said helping him up from the couch. Briell continued to laugh at the awkward scene.

"What did I miss?" Thadd asked groggily. Squirt looked at Thadd's drunken face and shook his head.

"Bro, why are you hard is a better question." Squirt asked as they walked towards the door.

"Bye." The three girls sang in unison waving at them.

"You're definitely going to see some things online now." Squirt shook his head, looking back at the three girls.

CHAPTER 4

B riell's phone began vibrating on his nightstand. He tried his best to ignore it. He had a serious hangover; his head was pounding. Suddenly, his room door opened, and he heard Squirt's voice.

"Bro, you are not going to believe this. But before I show you, I just want you to know I didn't do this." Squirt warned.

"What are you talking about, Squirt?" Briell said in a raspy tone. Squirt grabbed Briell's tablet and went to his Facebook page.

"OM fucking G, do you see all of these friend requests? It's over 500." Squirt exclaimed.

"What? Hold up, let me see it." He grabbed the tablet from Squirt's hands to look for himself. "What the fuck?"

"Damn, bro, do you see all these baddies requesting to be your friend?" Squirt said looking over Briell's shoulder.

"How is this possible?" Briell said, shaking his head in amazement.

"That's why I came over here. I've been calling and texting you for the last hour. Go to my page." Briell scrolled over to Squirt's page. "You see this YouTube link? Apparently, Deek had someone filming highlights of his party last night." He explained.

Briell clicked the link, and they both screamed in unison, "Oh, shit."

"No way, man. There's no way this video has so many views already." Briell said.

"Dawg, if the video reaches a million, you're going to go viral." Squirt exclaimed.

"How can this be possible? I know Vanessa Starr is popular, but six-hundred and forty-eight thousand views?" Briell shook his head in disbelief. The video was titled, "*Help JaBriell Gibson Find Love.*" Briell was in awe.

"Well, click play. I want to see again." Squirt chimed in.

Briell clicked play, and Vanessa Starr popped up for her usual blog. She was well known for airing the latest dirt and gossip on stars and regular people alike. Deek's wild parties were discussed on her blogs before, but this one was by far the biggest party yet.

"*What's up, my peeps? This is your girl Vanessa Starr of V.S. Entertainment. Ladies, this segment is all about you today. We have a hot man who is looking for love. And, when I say he's hot, he's hot.*" She said displaying a pic of Briell.

"*Ladies, this is JaBriell Gibson, he's twenty-five years old, born and raised in Tampa, Florida. He is the owner of a sandwich shop in the Town and Country area. He has his own money, money, money, ladies. He recently got dumped by his long-time girlfriend. They were high school sweethearts. I wouldn't have given up this piece of candy. Sources tell me she's the only chick he's ever dated or slept with.*" She finished before fanning herself.

"*I'm getting hot just thinking about the fresh meat. My sources have also said that he's a good person, a family man, and knows how to treat a woman. Check out this clip of him and his boys partying last night at one of Deek's wild parties.*" The video clip began to play following her commentary. The clip showed Squirt and Thadd walking in. It went on to show the announcement that Squirt made on the mic, and the girls giving Briell a lap dance. When the clip ended, the video flashed back to Vanessa who was holding a shot glass filled with Ciroc.

"*I'll take a shot for you, JaBriell.*" She said as she drank the shot.

"*Oh, and ladies, I just got a text from my source. They asked his ex why she broke up with him. She says, and I quote, 'Sometimes people just grow apart from one another. JaBriell is a great guy, I just needed a break.*" Vanessa paused for a minute to take another shot and then continued.

"*Well, honey, I wouldn't have let good man like JaBriell get away, but to each his own. I always say there are still good men in the world. JaBriell, I hope you can find love, again. I'm rooting for you. Ladies, JaBriell's Instagram and Facebook information is listed on the screen below. Hit him up and see if he's ready to start dating again. This is your girl Vanessa Starr, and I'll see you next time on 'What's Hot in the Streets.'*" She finished as the video ended abruptly.

"How did she know so much about me?" JaBriell wondered aloud.

"Don't look at me. I didn't tell her shit." Squirt said with his hands raised in surrender. Briell's phone continued to vibrate from all the Facebook and Instagram notifications.

"What are you going to do? I know you're not over Vonne, but at least check your DM's out and accept your friend requests." Squirt suggested.

"This is crazy, bro." Briell shook his head still in disbelief.

For the next hour, Briell accepted friend requests and checked out some of his DM's. He read all the messages yet didn't respond to anyone. He spent his day wondering what to do. Briell wasn't thirsty, especially for women. He decided he need time to sort things out, so he stayed home for the rest of the day, just chilling and contemplating.

When morning came JaBriell decided it was time to get back to work. He got dressed and went to his sandwich shop early to make sure everything was in order. London came in, followed by another employee, Chantel. They opened the shop up like any regular day. A few hours passed and JaBriell decided it was time to get out of the office and go for a quick run.

"I'll be back. I'm going to the bank to get some change." He announced. On the way to the car, he decided to go to Chick-fil-A as well. It didn't take him very long to run his errands and head back to the shop. When he pulled into the plaza, he noticed a small crowd of ten to fifteen people inside the sandwich shop. He pulled around the back of the building and walked through the back door. Once inside his office he began looking at the surveillance videos. The shop was filled with women, beautiful women at that. London walked into Briell's office, a few minutes after he arrived. He knew Briell was back because a bell sounded when he entered the back door.

"Excuse me, Jabriell, at least eight women have asked for you. What do you want me to tell them?" He asked looking baffled.

"Tell them I'm not here, and if it gets too busy, I'll see if I can get someone to come in and help manage the crowd." Briell said.

"You're a lucky man, JaBriell." London said with a smile.

"Thank you. Now get back out there. Chantel needs you." The lunch time rush was booming. The line was out the door. Not only were women flocking to the store, but men who worked in the area also. Briell's video had gone viral, and all the women who came to his shop wanted to see him. Many of them posted their food on social media as well. He asked Thadd to come in and help him out. It was summer, so he didn't have any classes to teach.

Before long, the day came to an end and Briell began prepping for the rest of the week. He made a few calls to order more meat and Cuban bread, along with fresh veggies. He had to pay an extra fee to have everything delivered early before the shop opened the following day. The shop made more money in a day, than it had since it opened. Briell was so consumed by work, he still hadn't responded to any of the women flooding his DM, but for some reason it made them want him more.

CHAPTER 5

The next day came, and business hadn't slowed down one bit. Briell was at the shop bright and early. He remained tucked away in the back, away from the crowd. In his mind he thought the instant fame and notoriety would soon blow over. His phone rang snapping him out of his thoughts. He looked down at the screen and saw it was his mother. Briell hadn't spoken to his mom or dad about what was going on.

"Hello, hey ma." He answered.

"Baby, they're talking about you on *The View*." She exclaimed with excitement.

"What's *The View*,' Ma?" he asked confused.

"Boy, turn to channel four right now." Briell grabbed the remote from the end of his desk and turned the television to Channel four just as his mother said. There was a group of four women discussing the party and helping him to find love. In the background they flashed footage of the party also.

"Oh my God, son, you're a celebrity. How did this happen?" His mom asked enthusiastically.

"It's a long story, Ma. We'll talk about it when I get home." He dismissed.

"Ok, baby. I'll talk to you later. I have to call your father and your aunt and tell them my baby is a celebrity." She said proudly.

"Ok, Ma." Briell said just before ending the call. Within seconds his phone was ringing again. This time it was a number he didn't recognize.

"Hello, this is JaBriell Gibson." He answered professionally.

"Hello, Mr. Gibson. My name is Angela Curtis with High Rise Productions. We produce popular reality shows, perhaps you may have heard of one of them."

"Hey, Mrs. Curtis. How can I help you?"

"My bosses are interested in doing a reality show based on you finding love. We're willing to pay you top dollar to sign with us. Are you willing to meet with us tomorrow? We would love to discuss what we have planned." Angela asked quickly.

"Um, okay. I'll be free after four." He answered a bit taken abet.

"Great, I'll call you when we arrive in Tampa. I look forward to meeting you, Mr. Gibson."

"I look forward to meeting you, too." JaBriell returned.

"Have a great night." Angela finished before she ended the call. JaBriell immediately googled High Rise Productions. He couldn't believe how many shows they had produced. Excited he dialed Squirts number.

"What up, my bro?" Squirt answered.

"You're not going to believe what I'm about to tell you." Briell responded.

"What happened now?" Squirt replied.

"My mom called me freaking out and screaming that Eve and Whoopi and whoever else is on the show *"The View"* were talking about me today. They showed the footage from the party. You were right, when you said it would get crazy if the video went viral. Well, apparently it did. Not only were the ladies of *"The View"* discussing me, but a woman by the name of Angela Curtis just contacted me. She's an associate with High Rise Productions, and they are flying in tomorrow to have a meeting with me about a reality TV show based on me finding love.

"Get the fuck out of here, bro." Squirt screamed into the phone.

"No bullshit, bro, and they want to pay me. We're going to be celebrities for real." Squirt screamed into the phone again. Briell just laughed at him.

"You and Thadd meet me at the crib around five-thirty to six this evening. My mom wants me to explain everything that's going on, I need you'll with me so we can make a decision on what I should do."

"We will be there, bro." Squirt agreed. When they hung up Briell was left staring into space. He couldn't believe all the attention he was getting.

By evening, JaBriell was grateful the day had drawn to a close. He got in the car and headed to his parents' home. When he arrived, he was quite surprised to see, Thadd and Squirt were already in the driveway waiting for him. He parked his car and got out to greet them.

The three of them dapped and hugged Briell, before going inside in the house. Both of Briell's parents were at home, along with Jassy.

"What's up, Ma? I'm home." Briell called out.

"We're in the kitchen, Briell. Your sister is helping me cook you some fried chicken." She called back out to him. Briell smiled and looked at his boys as they walked towards the 7kitchen. "Oh, Lord."

"My favorite brother." Jassy squealed as Briell and his friends entered the kitchen.

"I'm your only brother, and why are you being so nice to me? You usually punch me as soon as you see me." Briell teased.

"Since you're famous, can buy me a Mac notebook?"

"I'm not famous, Jassy." Briell shook his head at her thoughts.

"Yes, you are. Mommy said your picture was on a TV show, and they were talking about you. So, I want the new Mac notebook with a pink cover." She insisted.

"Jassy, leave your brother alone and come finish helping me. Hello, Thadd and Carlos."

"Hey, Mrs. Gibson." They spoke in unison.

"Are you all staying for dinner?" Stephanie asked turning to Squirt and Thadd. They looked at Briell for reassurance.

"Yeah, ma, they're staying. I need to talk to you and pops about something, and I wanted them to be here so we could all discuss things. Briell spoke up.

"Ok, honey. Y'all alright?" She asked looking at the three of them.

"Yeah, Ma, we're good. I'm going to go and change out of these work clothes. We'll be back down in a minute."

"Take your time, since Thadd and Carlos are eating with us, I'm going to fry some more chicken." She returned as the three of them turned to leave the kitchen.

When they arrived upstairs, Briell went into the bathroom to take a shower while Thadd and Squirt played NBA 2K on the PlayStation. Thirty minutes later, Jassy busted into Briell's bedroom.

"Y'all need to come eat, and don't take a long time because I didn't help cook all that food for it to get cold." Thadd and Squirt laughed at Jassy's comment as soon as she finished.

"There's my sister. I knew that niceness would be gone soon." Briell added as Jassy headed back downstairs.

"I told them Momma, but they're playing that game." Jassy reported as she reached the kitchen.

Not even five minutes passed, and Stephanie walked over to the stairs and yelled, "Y'all come down here and eat. Briell, you know how I am when I cook."

"We're coming now, Ma." Briell retorted as they headed downstairs. Even Thadd and Squirt knew Briell's mom didn't play. When they reached downstairs, Briell's dad was standing up watching ESPN.

"What's up, Pops?" Briell greeted.

"Hey, Mr. Gibson. What's going on?" Squirt greeted as each of they gave Mr. Gibson some dap.

"What y'all think Bron gon' do in this game? He needs some help, and Magic leaving isn't helping at all."

"They definitely need to make some changes, because Golden State going hard again this year. I don't think Houston is going to beat them, they're too strong." Squirt added.

"Squirt, you're right. I'm not a Golden State fan, but I have to give credit where it's due, those boys are strong." Mr. Gibson replied.

"I don't care if Golden State win again, I'm still a LeBron fan. The Lakers need to tighten up." Thadd chimed in.

"You feel me?" Briell said offering Thadd some dap for his comment.

"Can y'all come eat, please?" Stephanie urged.

"Ok, Baby. We're coming now." Mr. Gibson said as he put down the remote, and they headed into the dining room. Dinner was spread on the table and Jassy was already seated. Mr. Gibson pulled the chair out for Stephanie and gave her a kiss on the cheek.

"The food looks great, baby." He complimented.

"Daddy, I helped too." Jassy interjected.

"You did, Pumpkin? Well, let me give you some kisses too." He said before giving her a bunch of kisses and tickling her as she laughed.

"Let's bow our heads." He said as he took his seat and began to pray. When the prayer ended, they began passing the dishes around the table.

"I want two legs, Daddy." Jassy said looking over his shoulder.

"Ok, Pumpkin." He said putting two chicken legs on her plate. The conversation at the table was at a minimum as everyone enjoyed their dinner.

"Baby, is that all you're going to eat? The food is really good." Mr. Gibson said as Stephanie finished eating and placed a napkin on her plate.

"Yes, I had a piece of chicken and some Macaroni and cheese before we ate, so I'm good. I'm going to go and get Jasmine's bath ready. Briell, when you'll are done, rinse the dishes and put them in the dishwasher, and then we'll all sit in the living room and talk." She instructed standing up from the table.

"Ok, Ma." Briell said as Stephanie prepared to exit the dining room.

"Thadd, you and Carlos can help clean up the table." She added.

"Yes, ma'am." The two of them said in unison.

She kissed Mr. Gibson and then said, "Come on, Jassy. Let's get you cleaned up." Jazzy followed her mom's lead upstairs. The men continued their conversation about sports. Stephanie returned a short time later with a glass of wine and joined the guys in the living room.

"What's going on? Why are they talking about you on *The View*?'" Stephanie inquired.

"Well, as you'll know, me and Vonne broke up a couple weeks ago. Last week we went to a party." Briell spoke.

"We were trying to clear his mind of the breakup." Squirt added.

"Mmmhhh continue, JaBriell." Stephanie sighed a bit.

"Deek had a big party at his house, and during the party Squirt made an announcement that I'm single now, and everyone took a shot for me." Briell went on.

"That was the video they showed on 'The View.'" Stephanie added as she put together the pieces of the puzzle.

"Yes, Deek had someone filming the party, and a blogger named lady Vanessa Starr put the video on her YouTube and blog site. She's popular and her show gets tons of views and subscribers, so the video went viral. Women started contacting me on Facebook and Instagram. I also received a call from a company called High Rise Productions, who produce reality TV shows. They want to do a reality show about me finding love again. I agreed to a meeting. They're flying in tomorrow to meet me, and I don't know what to do. They're willing to pay me, for the opportunity." Briell finished and took a breath.

"Baby, are you saying that these people want you to be a reality television star? Have you even researched this company?" Stephanie asked quickly. Thadd handed her his phone to show her High Rise's website.

"Damn, they've produced all these shows?" She responded scanning through the list of shows previously produced.

"Yeah, Mama. This is real."

"Let me get this straight. You and Vonne broke up, and Squirt told everyone at a party, then a woman by the name of Vanessa Starr put the video on her blog site, which caused everyone to become interested in you finding love again?" Mr. Gibson said, still taken abet by all JaBriell had said.

"Let me see the video Vanessa Starr made." Briell quickly showed his mom and pops the YouTube video.

"Wow these people are really interested into you, Baby. How did they find out all that information on you?"

"I don't have the slightest clue. I don't know how they got in contact with Vonne, either." Briell shrugged.

"Damn, Son." Mr. Gibson smiled widely "My boy is going to be on T.V." He gave Briell some dap and then continued pumping him up, "Boy, you're going to be big time."

"He's already Instagram and Facebook famous." Squirt said enthusiastically.

"Women have been coming to the sandwich shop in droves to see him. He's been in his hiding out in his office avoiding them." Thadd added.

"Is this true, son?" Stephanie inquired looking over at Briell.

"Yeah, I had to hire Thadd the past two days to help out, it's been so busy." He answered.

"All of this because that damn Vanessa Starr posted that video on YouTube. I don't know, baby. These reality shows can get crazy. We've all seen them. I just don't know if I want you to go through that."

"Baby, it's his decision, and I think he should do it, take advantage of the opportunity. Plus, he will be getting paid. Who knows what other opportunities and doors may open from him doing this show." Mr. Gibson challenged his wife.

"These women only want him because he's a good man and has his shit together. I don't want any of these sack chasers trying to ruin that or use him." Stephanie said passionately.

"Baby, we've raised a good man. People need to know that there's still good black men out there. He could change black men's lives. It will allow the world to see something different. This doesn't have to be a negative thing."

"JaBriell, what do you want to do?" Stephani asked with her hand propped under her chin.

"Honestly, I want to do the show, especially if they're paying. It would be great publicity for my shop. There's a lot of good that can come out of this."

"Yeah, and a lot of bad can come out of this, too. But you're grown, and it's your decision. Me and your father will be behind you one hundred percent like we have always been."

"Will you all attend the meeting with me? Once we hear what they have planned, I will make my decision."

"Ok, baby, we'll be there." Stephanie agreed immediately.

"You know we got your back, Bro." Thadd said also.

"Definitely." Squirt shook his head in agreement.

CHAPTER 6

B riell decided to have Angela and her associates meet him at his parent's house. Angela didn't mind where the meeting took place. All she needed was for him to agree to the show and sign the contract so her bosses would be pleased with her. Angela and Maria were amazed at how beautiful Tampa was.

"This is beautiful." Angela said amazed by the scenery as they drove to Briell's home.

"I was thinking the same thing. It's the total opposite of the streets of New York." Maria agreed.

"Dillard, how long before we arrive?" Angela asked leaning forward.

"The GPS says we are seven minutes away. We're close." He returned. Angela picked up her cell phone and called Aaron.

"We will be arriving in seven minutes." Angela informed Aaron.

"Ok, are we going to an office building? This looks pretty residential to me." Aaron said observing the area.

"Your guess is as good as mine, Aaron."

"Okay," he retorted.

Once they hung up Maria began to mock Aaron, "Are we going to a building? This looks residential to me." She scoffed. Maria and Dillard laughed.

"He's so uppity and bourgeois, it makes me sick." Angela added. Aaron was one of High Rise's lawyers. He wasn't pleased he had to fly down to Tampa unexpectedly. When they arrived in Tampa, he had his own town car waiting for him. He also told Angela soon as the client signed the paperwork he was heading back to New York. Angela didn't care if he stayed or left. She preferred the latter.

"Look at those palm trees, and the houses are so beautiful, here." Maria admired as the passed an enormous public pool filled with kids. Two minutes later, arrived at JaBriell's parent's home. He came outside and waved to let them know they were at the right place.

"JaBriell, so nice to finally meet you." Angela greeted as she walked up and shook his hand.

"It's a pleasure to meet you as well. How was your flight?" JaBriell inquired as he welcomed them inside.

"It was good flight, hardly any turbulence. It's so beautiful here. It's always good to get away from the noisy, busy streets of New York." Angela answered.

"Hello, Angela. I'm Stephanie, JaBriell's mother, and this is his father, Jamal" Stephanie said with a smile.

"And who is this pretty lady?" Angela asked looking at Jassy who was smiling sweetly.

"I'm Jassy. JaBriell's my big brother." She answered politely.

"So nice to meet you, Jassy. I'm Angela, this is Maria, Dillard, and Aaron." Angela said introducing the rest of the crew.

"Are you going to make my brother a T.V. star?" Jassy asked looking up at Angela. Everyone laughed aloud.

"I hope so." Angela nodded her head. She knew if JaBriell wasn't ready for television, his little sister surely was.

"You'll come in and have a seat." Stephanie waved them further into the house.

"Can I get you all something to drink? We have bottled water, juice, soda, wine, alcohol." Jamal offered as they took a seat.

"I'll take some wine, red if you have it." Angela said promptly.

"My kind of girl." Stephanie winked.

"I'll have some wine also." Maria said.

"Anything with alcohol in it, preferably white." Dilliard chuckled.

"I'll have a bottled water, please." Aaron added.

"I'll be right back." Jamal said as he turned and headed towards the kitchen.

"Where are my manners? This is Thadd and Carlos, JaBriell's best friends, and this is Tracy, our attorney. We figured if JaBriell considered being a part of your show, he would have to sign a contract. So, to keep him safe, and to give us a full understanding, we invited Tracy in on the meeting."

"Smart woman." Aaron observed.

"Thank you, Aaron. Jassy go upstairs and play. Say good-bye to everyone." Stephanie said shoeing Jassy away.

"Aye, Briell, come and give me a hand." Jamal yelled from around the corner.

"Okay, Pops." JaBriell got up immediately and went to lend his dad a hand.

"Angela, I hope you don't mind us having the meeting at our house. We wanted to let you know Briell is really a family man. We have no influence on the decision he makes about the show, we're just here for support." Stephanie said. She could be outspoken especially when it came to her children.

"Family is important. I'm happy to know JaBriell has a family that supports him." Angela smiled.

"We have so many clients who don't live up to the facade they put on. This feels real and sincere." Maria shared.

"I agree." Dilliard stated. Jamal and JaBriell returned to the living room with a tray full of glasses and two bottles.

"Red wine for the ladies, and Ciroc for the guys." Jamal announced.

"I'll be right back." Briell walked into the kitchen and then returned with a bucket of ice and two bottled waters. "Here are some waters for the attorneys." Everyone in the room shared a quick laugh as he handed them the bottled water.

"When this meeting is over, I will definitely take some wine." Tracy chuckled. Jamal took the liberty of pouring everyone a drink.

"Alright Angela, let's get down to business." JaBriell said taking a seat.

"Absolutely." Angela agreed.

Angela began pitching the show without further ado. They talked for about forty minutes. JaBriell was impressed. He and his mother asked questions about different matters. They discussed all the details including how much JaBriell would be paid and the logistics of the show. Aaron and Tracy had a few words regarding the terms of the contract, but they were minor.

"JaBriell, what do you think?" Angela asked as the talks concluded.

"If Tracy feels the contract is good and the money is fair, I have no problem being a part of the show. I do have one request, though. When you pick the girls for the show, I would like them to be selected from my Instagram and Facebook requests. I know many television shows use actors and models, but I want the women to have an actual interested in me." JaBriell explained.

"You want it to be real, and I respect that, and I think we can all agree to your request." Maria nodded her head.

'That's definitely not a problem." Angela agreed looking over at Aaron. "Me, Maria, and Dillard will pick the girls tonight. We will meet with you tomorrow to show you the selection. JaBriell, things are going to happen fast once you sign the contract. *Good day America'* would like to interview you, and that will take place in two days. This will give America a chance to hear from you and your thoughts on the show." Angela paused to allow JaBriell an opportunity to take everything in.

"After that, we will shoot a pilot for the show. We will film you at the beach house in Clearwater. The girls will be there as well. We will start filming in exactly two weeks. The show will air live. We will additionally film your dates and activities throughout the week. Viewers will be able to chime in through Facebook, Instagram, and

Twitter. We will choose date locations and restaurants, once you find someone you really like, you can choose where you'd like to take them. If there are no further questions, we will give Aaron and Tracy a few minutes to make sure everything is in order with the contract. You can also take a moment to discuss things with your family and friends while we wait.

"Me and Aaron are good, but I would like to speak with JaBriell privately." Tracy spoke out.

"We can go into the kitchen." Stephanie said standing up from her chair.

"Can I get you all any other refreshments?" Jamal offered.

"No, Thank you." Angela said politely as JaBriell, his parents and Tracy exited the room.

"JaBriell, how are you feeling about everything? I know this is a lot to take in?" Tracy asked.

"Actually, I'm good, but I'm kind of nervous about the *'Good Day America'* show."

"I will attend the show if you need me to. I will assist in making sure they ask you the appropriate questions. The contract is great, you have no issues there. I think it's a great opportunity financially. Your life will change socially, though. Everyone will know who you are." Tracy explained.

"Are you ready for that, son?' Jamal asked.

"I'm ready, pop." JaBriell smiled wide.

"Alright, let's get your signature on this contract and get you paid." Tracy said as they prepared to walk out of the kitchen.

"Angela, he's ready to sign." Tracy announced as they reentered the living room.

"Welcome aboard." Angela said proudly as she shook JaBriell's hand.

Maria and Dillard stood also and followed suit shaking JaBriell's hand. Angela placed the contract before JaBriell who quickly signed it. Aaron pulled a check from his briefcase and handed it to JaBriell quicker than the ink could dry.

"Whew." JaBriell remarked looking down at the check and then over at Thadd and Squirt, "It's on, baby." Everyone laughed while giving one another hugs and dap.

"It was nice meeting you folks. I have a plane to catch. "Aaron said as he began gathering his belongings. He shook JaBriell's hand and again and said, "Good luck on finding love. Angela, I'll see you back in New York."

"Have a safe flight." Angela responded. The rest of the room said their good-byes to Aaron as he left the house.

"I'll have that drink now." Tracy said to Stephanie who was standing nearby.

"I'll have one, myself." Stephanie laughed.

"Well, everyone, we would love to stay and drink, but we have work to do. JaBriell, can you write down your Facebook and Instagram info along with the passwords, for us? You can change them tomorrow. We won't spy around." Angela assured him.

"It's cool, Angela. I have nothing to hide." JaBriell said as he did as Angela requested.

"Here's my personal cell phone number. If you can't get in touch with me, here's Maria's number. Call us anytime. We're on the same team now." Angela said handing JaBriell her and Maria's business cards.

"Thanks for everything, Angela."

"No problem, JaBriell." Angela smiled she had landed a new client and was more than sure this show would be a hit.

"You're about to change my life." JaBriell smiled back while hugging her.

"Stephanie, if I had time, I would have a drink with you, girl. But we have to handle some business."

"I understand. We will pour one up next time." Stephanie said warmly as she walked the three of them to the door.

"Give me that check, boy. Me and your father are going to make sure this goes in your bank account tonight." Stephanie said the moment she walked back into the living room.

"Yeah, you, Thadd and Squirt aren't about to party on this check. We're gone put this into your savings acount." Jamal added.

Briell handed the check over to his mom, and she grabs her keys swiftly, "We'll be back. Go ask your sister what she wants to eat for dinner. We will bring y'all some food back." Stephanie shouted behind her as she walked out the door. As soon as his parents left, Thadd and Squirt start dancing and rapping a song, and then JaBriell joined in.

"We're hitting the strip club tonight." Squirt said. Thadd began slapping an imaginary ass and rapping Juvenile's *"Back That Ass Up"* song. Squirt grabbed the Ciroc bottle and 3 shot glasses. He filled each of them up and handed them to JaBriell and Thadd.

"To my boy Briell finding love and having his own show on prime-time television. I'm proud of you, man." Squirt congratulated.

"Me too, bro." Thadd agreed.

"And if it wasn't for me, your ass wouldn't be famous right now." Squirt laughed,

"I can't front, if you would have never shouted me out at Deek's party, none of this would have happened." JaBriell said graciously. They lifted their shot glasses in the air and then took a shot.

"Yo, no cap, Maria is super bad." Thad interjected.

"Boy, I was thinking the same thing." Squirt chuckled.

"Too bad she isn't a part of the show." Thadd shook his head.

"She is tough, but I can't talk to her. She's like one of my bosses." Briell said.

"I wouldn't care if she was my boss. I would be like whoop, whoop, pull over, that ass too phat, whoop, whoop." Squirt joked. They laughed in unison as Thadd poured another round of shots.

CHAPTER 7

I t was almost one in the morning, Briell, Thadd and Squirt were in Hollywood Nights strip club. They were having a blast. Briell felt normal. Nobody knew him, especially the strippers. The boys were tipsy. Briell decided to send a video of them wilding out to Maria. She was around their age. He figured she would still be awake. Once he pressed send, he sent another text, saying: *"Just having fun before the show starts."*

Within a few minutes, she texted him back, *"You're having more fun than me."* She followed up with another text that read: *"Don't forget to take a good shower, to wash all that booty juice off you."* Briell read her text and started laughing almost instantly.

He quickly responded: *"Lol, booty juice. How did the selection go?"*

"It went good, we picked fifteen girls and five alternates."

"Cool, don't stay up late. You have work tomorrow, Boss." JaBriell replied.

"Whatever. And it's Mrs. Boss." She shot back. *"Don't get fired on your first day for being late, get some rest."* She added.

"Lol, I am. We're about to leave in a minute to go and get something to eat, then it's a wrap." JaBriell texted.

"Where are you'll going to eat?" She inquired.

"IHOP," He replied.

"Bring me some pancakes, eggs and bacon, extra syrup." she wrote.

"Are you capping?" He inquired.

"Huh?" Maria replied confused.

"I mean joking, or are you serious?" JaBriell smiled while texting her back.

"Oh yes, I'm serious. We're at the Marriott Suites downtown, room five-twenty-six." she answered quickly.

"Ok, leaving now. Give me about forty-minutes." JaBriell responded before telling Thadd and Squirt he was leaving.

"What the hell, bro? The night is still young. I've got more ones to throw." Squirt said.

"And we still have Ciroc left in our bottle." Thadd added on.

"Something came up. I have an early morning tomorrow. My Uber is on the way already. I'll hit you two up in the morning" He gave his boys some dap and a man hug headed out the door before they asked anymore questions. He didn't keep things from his boys, but he felt he should keep the fact that he was taking Maria some food to himself.

He arrived at the hotel and texted Maria, letting her know he was there.

"Send me a text when you get off the elevator, everyone is asleep." She replied.

When he got off the elevator, he did as she asked. He walked down the hallway and saw Maria coming out of the room. When she saw him, she smiled and waved her hand. Briell couldn't believe how beautiful she was. Her hair was natural with the curls. Her smile was pretty, her skin tone was light, and her body was perfect. She had a white tank top on, showing her breast size. She also had on some short Syracuse orange and white shorts on. Briell couldn't keep his eyes off the print between her legs as he walked towards her.

"Hey," She sang as she hugged him. The scent of her lotion had him in a trance. She "Thank you for bringing me some food. I was starving. We didn't eat anything since earlier today. We were working on the show, all night."

"It's no problem. I'm just glad I was able to get you something. Oh, I got you extra bacon, too. A portion is only three little strips, and that's not enough." Briell flashed a smile.

"Thank you so much. "Maria said as they stared at one another. She paused for a minute and then began to speak again, "If it wasn't so late, I would invite you in. Dillard is sleeping on the pull-out sofa."

"It's cool, I understand. I'll see you tomorrow, Mrs. Syracuse, aka Mrs. Boss." Briell smiled big. As the two of them shared a laugh.

"That's right, home of the Orangemen, baby." Maria cheered.

"I see you." He shook his head still admiring her.

"Briell, Thanks again. I'll see you tomorrow." Maria said as she turned to open the room door. Briell shook his head from left to right. *"Damn, Maria, all that booty back there."* He thought to himself. She noticed him lusting after her and smiled.

"Go and wash that booty juice off you, Stinky.

"Whatever." Briell laughed a bit as he stepped on to the elevator. When he reached the lobby, he ordered himself another Uber while thinking about Maria. JaBriell was trying his best to put Maria out of his thoughts. He needed to prepare for the show. Within a few minutes he was home. He took a nice long shower and headed to bed shortly after.

CHAPTER 8

JaBriell woke up around seven-thirty in the morning feeling good. He hardly felt the effects of his late night out. He was up and ready to start his day. Once he got out the bed his first stop was in his sister's room.

"Big head, get up." He shook, her eyes slowly began to open.

"Get up and get ready." He informed her as she stared at him groggily.

"Get ready for what? It's the summer, I'm out of school." She spoke still half asleep.

"Just get up." He tickled her. "You need to brush your teeth because your breath is kicking."

"My breath don't stink, yours do." Jassy snapped back at him.

Briell blew his hot breath on her and laughed. Jassy quickly replied, "I'm melting, I'm melting." Both she and Briell laughed at her comment.

"Alright, since you want to stay in the bed, I guess I won't buy you anything. See you later." Briell said as he pretended to walk out of the room

"I'm up, I'm up."Jassy threw back the covers and leaped out of bed.

"Hurry up and get dressed, and don't forget to brush your teeth." Briell instructed her.

"I won't. Can I wear whatever I want?" Jassy asked.

"I don't care, just hurry up." Briell said as he walked back to his bedroom. Jassy had never dressed herself, before. Their mom usually picked out her clothes, but Stephanie was still in the bed. She told her employees that she would arrive at the daycare around noon,today. Thirty minutes later, Briell and Jassy knocked on their mom's bedroom door.

"Ma, me and Jassy are about to hang out. We're about to go eat some breakfast." He told her.

"Why are y'all up so early, and where are y'all going?" she asked still half asleep.

"Wherever she wants to go. She's the boss today." JaBriell smiled.

"Why didn't you two invite me?" She asked, her eyes scanned over Jassy's outfit, and then she frowned. "Jasmine what do you have on?

"Clothes, Mama."

"I let her pick out her own clothes, today." JaBriell said looking at Jassy's outfit as well.

"I can see that." Stephanie sat up in the bed. "Lord have mercy. Come on, Jassy, let me find you something to wear." She said throwing back the covers.

"Ma, we don't have time for all of that, she's good. I'm letting her have her independence." JaBriell said smoothing things over.

"Shut up, boy. You will not have my baby looking crazy, and I need to do her hair. It won't take long." She said as she took Jassy by the hand and led her into her room. In twenty minutes flat she had Jassy looking fresh.

"Briell, I'm ready to go." Jassy said running down the stairs.

"It's about time, big head." Briell teased.

"You two be careful, and don't let her sit in the front seat." Stephanie warned.

"Alright, ma. We will, and I got it." Briell said before kissing his mother on the cheek and taking Jassy by the hand.

"What kind of music do you want to listen to?"

"I want to listen to Ella Mai." Jassy said confidently. She loved the song *"Boo'ed up"*.

"Ok, and what do you want eat for breakfast?"

"McDonald's. Jassy said quickly.

"You always want McDonald's." JaBriell shook his head as he turned on Ella Mai and headed in the direction of McDonald's. When they arrived, they went inside and ordered their food. They took a seat at the table and sat down to eat. Jassy was full of energy and jokes, she had JaBriell laughing the whole time. He missed spending time with his sister. She was getting older and more independent.

They took a couple pics for Instagram and Facebook. His post read; *"Good morning, y'all. Hanging out with my little sister. We're about to do it big today."* Before they left McDonald's, he had over one hundred likes and sixty comments.

After McDonald's, they stopped by his sandwich shop. He had hired a new girl to help. He knew Thadd couldn't keep coming in to save him. Once everything was in order there, he left and took Jassy to Town and Country Mall. He bought her clothes and three pairs of shoes. He even bought her a necklace and bracelet. They both were fourteen carat gold. He told her she couldn't wear it every day because it was real gold, and she would lose it. He took a picture of her with all her shopping bags in her hands. His Instagram and Facebook likes, and comments were blowing up. All the women loved the fact that he was spending the day with his sister and spoiling her.

It was a little after eleven in the morning and Briell wanted to buy his mom something nice. He went to Macy's and got her a Pandora bracelet.

"You want to get some lunch before we go to another store?" Briell asked Jassy.

"Yeah, but we don't have to eat at McDonald's." Jassy answered sweetly.

"Thank God." Briell clapped. The two of them went to Red Lobster for lunch. They dined on all-you-can-eat shrimp. Shortly after they were seated Briell received a call from Angela.

"Hey, Briell, we were wondering if you will be home around three this afternoon."

"Yeah, I should be there. I'm taking Jassy to one more store." He answered.

"Your Instagram and Facebook pages are blowing up with the pics you're posting. These women love the fact that you're spending time with your sister. This makes them want you more." Angela gushed.

"I guess that's a good thing. It would be great for the show." Briell shrugged.

"Absolutely. We will see you around three." Angela confirmed again.

"Ok, see you guys this afternoon." Briell hung up the call and then called his mom to let her know Angela would be coming over. Once he was done, he gave Jassy the phone to check in with their mom.

"Hey, ma. I'm eating shrimp. "Jassy announced as she put the phone to her ear.

"Are you?" Stephanie answered.

"Yep, do you want me to bring you some?" Jassy asked.

"Yeah, bring me some. Are you having fun with your brother?"

"Yes, ma'am. He said we going to one more store. And we bought you a gift. I helped pick it out." Jassy said cutely.

"Aww that's so sweet, I'll see you'll in a little while. Put your brother back on the phone. Love you. "

"Love you too, Mama." She said before handing JaBriell the phone and continuing to eat her lunch.

"Baby, bring me some shrimp. I want some scampi, grilled, and shrimp pasta." Stephanie expressed as soon as JaBriell got on the phone.

"Ok." he answered as the finished their call.

When they finished eating at Red Lobster, they went to Walmart. He let Jassy pick out a new bike and helmet. He also got her a little flat screen TV with a DVD player. The TV was pink, and she picked out a bunch of DVDs to go along with it. After putting the items in the car and strapping the bike in the trunk, Briell and Jassy headed home. As he began driving, he looked in his rearview mirror, and saw Jassy was knocked out. Briell smiled at his sister. He felt good that he was able to spend the day with her.

"Can I ride my bike?" Jassy asked almost immediately as they arrived in the driveway.

"Yeah, I'll get out there with you. First, let's get all your stuff in the house and show Mama your clothes and the gift we got her. "JaBriell said as he began to unload the car.

"Ok." Jassy gathered her bags and helped Briell carry them inside, "Mama, look what I got." She exclaimed as soon as she laid eyes on her mother.

"Why'd you spoil this girl with all this stuff?" Stephanie asked as she scanned over all the bags they were carrying.

"'Because that's my homie." Briell said giving Jassy a high-five.

"Mama, we got you something, too." Jassy revealed handing her a Macy's shopping bag.

"I love it, I really do. Thank you, baby. "Stephanie said after opening the bag and box inside. She kissed Jasmine and then Briell. "Can I put it on now?" she asked.

"Yeah." They both exclaim in unison. Briell loved seeing his mother and sister happy. He really loved the two of them.

"Come on, Briell I want to ride my bike." Jassy said pulling Briell towards outside.

"Briell, I know you didn't buy this girl a new bike. She just got one last year." Stephanie said with her hands on her hips.

"That bike is old, Ma. She needed a new one." Briell explained.

"Get your helmet, and I'll be ready in a minute." Briell sent Jassy on her way, and then handed his mom her bag of food from Red Lobster. He sprinted up the stairs to drop his bags off in his room also. When he came back down the stairs his mom was going through the clothes, he bought Jassy.

He met Jassy at the door and the two of them went outside to play, he helped her ride her bike up and down the block. Twenty minutes later, Briell noticed a town car pulling into the driveway. He had totally forgot about the meeting with Angela. They parked, and Angela, Maria and Dillard exited the car.

"Hey, JaBriell." Angela spoke first.

"Hey, Angela. Hey, Maria. What's up, Dillard?" Briell greeted all three of them in sequence.

"Hi, Angela." Jassy squealed.

"Hello, Miss. Jasmine. I see your brother's teaching you how to ride your bike." Angela commented with a smile.

"Yeah, I only fell off twice. "Jassy said with pride.

"Yeah, she's getting the hang of it. Well, come on let's go in now. We will practice later. I'll set up your new TV and DVD player so you can watch a movie." JaBriell waved Jassy towards the house.

"Ok. I want to watch *'The Secret Life of Pets.'*"

"I love that movie." Maria added as they all walk inside the house.

"Ma, Mrs. Angela is here." Briell called out as they entered the house.

Briell led them into the living room and offered them something to drink.

"Hey, guys. Good to see you again." Stephanie said as she reached the living room where they were seated.

"Ma, can you get them something to drink? I'm going to set up Jassy's T.V. and DVD player. Maria, do you want to come and help me?" Briell asked.

"Sure." Maria agreed. Jassy grabbed her hand and walked upstairs beside her. "You want to see my room?"

"I sure do." Maria smiled as the three of them made it to the top of the stairs.

Meanwhile Stephanie was downstairs playing hostess to Angela and Dillard. "Angela and Dillard, would you two like to come into the kitchen with me? I'm pretty sure we can find something good to drink." Stephanie offered.

"I need one. We were up all night trying to find the perfect girls for JaBriell." Dillard said.

While upstairs in Jassy's room, Briell began hooking the DVD player and new television. Jassy was busy showing Maria her Barbie doll collection. Briell connected all the cords and popped in the movie.

"Alright, Jassy, your movie is on." Briell said excitedly.

"Can Maria watch it with me?" Jassy requested.

"Maybe next time. We have to go to a meeting now." Briell said letting Jassy down easy. Jassy looked sad as she sat on her bed and began to watch the movie.

"I'll tell you what, before I leave to go home to New York, I'll take all of us to see '*The Secret Life of Pets, Part 2*,' is that cool?" Maria offered hoping to cheer Jassy up.

"Ok, but don't forget." She hugged Maria and grabbed her baby doll before sitting in front of the television.

Maria and JaBriell walked downstairs, and he said, "She really likes you. She never likes anybody."

"Because I got the juice." Maria flexed a little bit.

"Oh, so you're dripping like that?" Briell teased.

"Drip, drip, drip." Maria shook her shoulders causing them to both laugh.

"Did you enjoy your food last night?" Briell asked.

"I did, thank you again." Maria answered sweetly. When they reached the bottom of the stairs Dillard was turning the corner, He quickly noticed their connection but decided not to say anything.

"Briell, your mother is trying to get us wasted already." Dillard said instead.

"Oh, yeah, she's good at that." Briell laughed.

They five of them walked into the living room and took a seat, Angela opened a folder and puts fifteen pictures of girls on the ottoman and five other pictures on the floor.

"Briell, these are the girls we picked, and these five are alternates. The alternates are here just in case you don't like one of these girls." Angela said, as Briell began to glance over the pictures.

For an hour, they viewed each of the pictures and told Briell what each girl does for a living, rather working or college student. Briell picked thirteen girls from the first pile of photos and two girls from the alternate stack. Once he made his choices, they began to discuss his appearance on, *"Good Day America."*

"Tomorrow, you have a full day. I booked you a room at the hotel we're staying at. You will ride in the town car with us. I've already spoke to Tracy. She will meet us there. Stephanie, if you and your husband or Jassy want to be there, we have all your names on the guest list. You will have access badges waiting for you. JaBriell, right after the show, we will head to Clearwater to get you prepped for the commercial. Remember, the girls will be there as well."

"I'm actually reaching out to them all right now. As of right now, we have nine that have confirmed to do the show and the commercial shoot." Maria added.

"Great. JaBriell, you need a nice suit, a casual outfit, and a pair of swim trunks. Also, we will have makeup and stylist available for you, but if you want to get a haircut by your own barber, that's fine with me. I just need you to be comfortable. And most importantly, I need you to stay calm. With everything going on, I don't need you to freak out." Angela said touching his shoulder.

"Baby, how are you feeling about everything?" Stephanie asked in a serious tone.

"I'm good, ma, I'm good. Angela, I won't let y'all down. I'm ready." Briell assured the two of them.

"Four more just confirmed for show and commercial shoot." Maria cheered eagerly.

"Great, everything's coming together. Dillard, make sure we have the confidentiality agreements for the girls to sign." Angela said.

"I'm on it." Dillard threw Angela a thumbs up.

"I'm going to go and pack. I'll be ready in about twenty minutes."

"Stephanie, can I speak to you in the kitchen. Plus, I want to get a refill."

"Yeah, girl. Come on, I need one, too." Stephanie said as she led Angela back into the kitchen.

"Stephanie, I give you my word, if he looks as if it's too much for him, I promise I will call you." Stephanie hugged Angela feeling reassured her son was in good hands.

"Thank you, Angela. Thank you for everything."

"No problem." Angela noticed tears in Stephanie's eyes, and she started to get emotional, too. "Girl, look at us. I need a drink now. This is a time for us to be happy. JaBriell will be fine."

Stephanie wiped her eyes and laughed, "Girl, you're right. This is supposed to be a happy time. I just get in my feelings just knowing all these women want my son, not for his heart but for all the attention he's getting." Stephanie said as she poured them another drink. "Has anyone found true love from a reality show?" She wondered aloud. Angela took a deep breath and looked at Stephanie. They both laughed heartily.

"I knew that shit was for ratings." Stephanie laughed some more.

"The juicier the show, the more ratings it gets. The more rachetness, the more ratings it gets. I'm a firm believer in the Lord. Whenever he's ready to send you the right person, that person will come in your life. And honestly, there's been some love connections from the show, but no marriages. I also feel JaBriell is different. You raised a good child. I mean, a young man that's only been with one partner, that's unheard of these days, especially for a man. So be proud of that." Angela encouraged, trying to look on the bright side of things.

"Amen, and I'll drink to that." Stephanie said as she raised her glass. They both laugh and sip on their wine.

"Do you have anyone special in your life?" Stephanie asked candidly.

"I had someone. He was supposed to be the one I married and had kids with, but I got this job and found myself being married to it. I had never made this kind of money before, and the more successful I became, the more money came with it, our relationship became one sided. He was home by himself, and I was working or out of town working, and his punk ass couldn't handle it. Years later, we got a divorce, and now I pay him alimony. I've dated, but nothing serious. I'm just going with the flow, girl. I'm forty-two years old. I still have time, but I will not rush into anything, and I'm damn sure not about to let another man make me think my success is the reason I don't have love."

"You're damn right." Stephanie agreed.

"What's your story? How did you get a good man like Jamal?" Angela inquired.

"Girl," She smiled at the thought of her husband. "We were high school sweethearts. I was the hood chick, and he was raised in a two-parent home with a big family. We ended up having JaBriell when I was seventeen. I hadn't even graduated from high school yet. He had got accepted to all these colleges to play football, but because I was pregnant, he chose USF, and we both went there, and his family helped with JaBriell when he was a baby. He never left me and Briell. He's always been a family man. That's why I think JaBriell is so family oriented. He gets that from his father. I worked my ass off and saved my money and opened a daycare after I got my degree. It's been successful. I'm grateful." Stephanie finished.

"That's a beautiful story, Stephanie. You're blessed." Angela said with a pat on the back.

"You're blessed too, girl. You're a successful black woman in a brutal industry, and you're running shit. Some men just can't handle that. But like you said, God got somebody for everybody. You'll get the right man, just hang in there." Stephanie encouraged Angela as well.

"Excuse me, Ms. Angela and Mrs. Stephanie, I just wanted to tell you everyone has confirmed for the show and commercial shoot. We're at one-hundred percent."

Angela smiled big; all her plans were coming together perfectly. "Yes, Great job, Maria. I need you to contact the property manager and let her know everything is on schedule for the villa, and have Dillard contact the filming company to make sure everything is on schedule as well. Also check on JaBriell to make sure he's good. Let him know the train is leaving in twenty minutes, and he needs to be on it."

"Yes, ma'am." Maria said turning on her heels and exiting the kitchen.

"She seems to be a good girl, works hard." Stephanie observed as Maria walked away.

"She is, and she does work hard. The damn girl will probably take my job. By then I should be behind a desk calling all the shots. She's young and ambitious. She reminds me of myself when I was her age. Poor girl works herself to death. She won't get a boyfriend. Hell, she won't even go on a date. I can understand not having a boyfriend, but sometimes a woman needs a date, a man to take her out, make her feel special, even get a little bit, feel me?"

"Girl, I do. That's why I married mine. Briell's about to leave, and Jassy is going with her Aunty tonight. I need my get right time, tonight." Stephanie said fanning herself.

"Girl, you bad." They both laughed again and continue to talk.

Maria walked upstairs and overheard Jassy laughing at the movie. She walked down the hall to Briell's room and knocked on the door softly. It was open. She walked in called out to him. She looked around at his room, and Briell came out of his bathroom with a towel on his head, drying off. He didn't hear or see Maria. She saw him and froze. He was wearing nothing but his boxer briefs. She felt her body get hot after seeing his abs and chiseled body. Her eyes stared at the bulge between his legs. He takes the towel from his face and saw Maria standing before him.

"I'm sorry. Angela sent me to let you know we were heading out in twenty minutes. Your door was open, and when I knocked, you didn't answer. So, I came in. I didn't know you were in the shower."

"It's cool. I'm just glad she sent you instead of Dillard." Briell smiled.

"Alright, see you in a minute. I'm going back downstairs." Maria exited the room, allowing Briell some privacy to get dressed.

CHAPTER 9

Briell was checked into his hotel room for the evening. He was relaxing, after looking over the women's photos, again. He took the liberty of checking out some of their Instagram and Facebook pages as well. He quickly realized a lot of the girls were not looking for love, they just wanted to be on T.V., which was cool with him. He picked up his phone sent a text to Maria: *"I'm bored. What you are you doing?"*

He then walked over to the mini bar and grabbed a Heineken and opened it. She soon texted back, *"Relaxing in the jacuzzi."*

JaBriell responded immediately asking; *"Do you want some company? Need to get out of this room for a minute."*

Maria texted back shortly later, *"Sure, but Dillard is here with me, Lol."*

Briell laughed and texted back; *"Oh, Lord. Lmao."*

Maria burst out laughing. She then texted back, *"Bring a bucket of ice. We're drinking too."*

He texted back; *"Who said I was coming?"*

She sent him a mad face emoji. Her last text prompted his to text back quickly, *"Where is the jacuzzi?"*

"By the workout area just before the pool." She replied along with a smiley face emoji.

Fifteen minutes later, Briell showed up with the bucket of ice. He made a drink for Maria and Dillard. They began talking about the girls they picked out for him and who they thought was sincere and who was chosen for their looks and or personality.

"Where's Angela?" Briell inquired.

"She's at the bar celebrating, probably with the manager that's been so nice to her." Dillard answered.

"Extremely nice." Maria added with a smirk. Her and Dillard started laughing.

"Celebrating what?" Briell asked confused.

"The show. That's her job. Hell, that's all of our jobs." Dillard said matter of factly.

"That's why we were having a drink, relaxing. Long as she's happy, we're happy." Maria said holding up her glass.

As they talked a hotel attendant walked in and replaced their towels with fresh ones. Him and Dillard looked at each other. When the guy left the area, Dillard said, "That's my cue. I will see you'll later. I'm about to have a celebration of my own." He winked getting out of the jacuzzi.

"You kids have fun." He waved behind him.

"Don't be all night. You know we have an early morning." Maria called behind him.

"Such a mother." Dillard joked.

"Whatever." She then looked at Briell and asked, "So are you going to get in?"

"Yeah. I just don't want to get in at the moment."

"You don't have to worry about Dillard. He stays in his lane. He's cool, trust me." She reassured him.

"I feel you, and I hate to be homophobic. Don't get me wrong, it doesn't bother me that he's homosexual, I just don't feel comfortable being in a jacuzzi with him. I mean I don't know him or his intentions, and I'm getting to know you. I just kick back and observe." Briell revealed.

"I like that about you. You're not all thirsty or arrogant. You carry yourself with class." Maria smiled digging JaBriell's style.

"I appreciate that. I can tell that you're observant too, and you're not like a lot of chicks out here." JaBriell said observing her also.

"What do you mean?" Maria said cocking her head to the side.

"I can tell you're about your business, you work hard, you're beautiful and you're down to earth. A lot of chicks that know they're pretty act stuck up, hard to hold conversations with. I just think you're really cool, and I'm glad we met."

"I'm glad we met, too." They look at each other, and Maria smiled and then looked away. "Can I ask you a question?"

"Yeah, go for it." Briell shrugged.

"You're a black man that owns a Cuban sandwich shop, I'm curious to know why?"

Briell laughed, then Maria laughed also, "I'm serious."

"When I was growing up, my mom would always take me to Joyce's Cuban Sandwich Shop. I loved those sandwiches, especially pressed. Tampa has a lot of places that make Cuban sandwiches. Some of them make good ones, and some of them make bad ones. I saved my money, I decided to invest in something I liked, so I opened a sandwich shop. Tampa has a huge Spanish community that loves Cuban sandwiches, just like blacks and whites. In the Town and Country area, they all order from my shop, especially now. I've gotten so much business I had to hire another worker." JaBriell explained.

"I'm part Spanish, so I know firsthand about Cuban sandwiches. Growing up in New York, we have a lot of sandwich shops that specialize in making Cuban sandwiches."

"You have to try my Cuban sandwich out before you leave." JaBriell added.

"I'm definitely going to have to see if it's official." Maria nodded her head.

"Is your mom Spanish or your dad?"

"My dad is Spanish, and my mom is a black woman from the Bronx." Maria answered proudly.

"The boogie down, huh?" Briell joked.

"Ok, I see you know the lingo. But yeah, I'm a BX girl all day, baby."

"I see that hood side of you coming out." Briell laughed.

Maria laughed and said, "I am so not hood. My dad was a dope boy. He moved us from the Bronx when I was little. The only reason I ever experienced that side of the tracks was because I have aunts and uncles who still live there. When my mom and dad would have date night or go out of town, I would stay with my Aunt Sheila. She stayed in the projects. It was different from Manhattan. My pops would hate for me to go there, but my mom would always tell him I needed to know who my real family was and where they came from. My dad doesn't have family like that, but he understood where my mom was coming from. Family is important. That's why I like you and your family. You're very family oriented. What you did with Jassy today was amazing. I wish I had an older brother to spoil me sometimes. My dad spoiled me, but it's not the same." Maria said revealing a bit more about herself.

"Yeah, me and Jassy are so far apart in age. When I was living in my own place, I didn't see her as much, I missed spending time with her. I needed her to know that her brother loves her and has her back. It's important to me that we have a genuine relationship. So can I ask you a question?"

"Of course." Maria said quickly.

"Do you have a boyfriend?"

"Oh, you're just going to come straight out with it, huh?" Maria chuckled.

"I mean, yeah, I want to know. You work for this big company, your job is demanding, and you travel a lot. So, I wonder how you balance a relationship with your job."

"I don't know about balancing a relationship because I don't have a boyfriend. I haven't had a boyfriend since college, and I received my degree three years ago. I'm twenty-four and single. Sometimes it sucks, but I love not having drama in my life. Sometimes men can be a distraction, especially the wrong man. If I'm in a relationship, I'm all the way in. I don't cheat, I'm not a hot girl, I don't give up my goodies like that. A lot of guys don't want to wait to get to know you, they just want to smash. I don't fall for that. Whenever God decides to bring the right man in my life, I'll be single."

They sat in silence for a minute or so, before Maria spoke again. "A job doesn't have anything to do with a relationship. If a man and woman truly love each other, they will do what they must, to make the relationship work, especially if God is involved. God can make anything possible; I truly believe that."

"I truly believe that, too." JaBriell agreed as he looked at Maria. "I also believe God brings people in your life for a reason."

Maria nodded and said, "This water feels so good, I can stay in it forever."

"Forever is a long time." JaBriell observed.

"You're right. That's why I'm about to get out. You want to get something to eat? I'm hungry."

"You stay hungry." Briell laughed.

"Shut up." Maria laughed hitting him with the towel. When she got out of the jacuzzi, JaBriell stared at her beautiful body. He felt himself getting excited. He couldn't believe how bad she was. In his eyes, Maria was perfect.

She pulled her bikini bottom out of her butt and noticed Briell looking at her. She smiled and then said, "Give me my towel, booty juice." He laughed and got out of the jacuzzi. When he got out of the jacuzzi, she saw him in slow motion as the water fell off him. She couldn't her eyes as they focused on his manhood sticking out of his swim trunks. Briell grabbed a towel and twisted it up and acted like he was going to pop her with it. She ran away from him. He chased her and then popped her on the butt with the towel.

"That hurt." She laughed and screamed while holding her butt.

"Awww, I sorry." She grabbed the towel from him, and then she twisted it up.

"Don't do it." He screamed. She starts chasing him around, and then she popped him on the thigh. He screamed and laughed. He turned around and grabbed her. They were both laughing as he held onto her. They stood frozen looking into one another's eyes. He moved her hair from her face, Briell was so gentle with her. He caressed her shoulders and then put his arms around her. They both moved in closer as their eyes were still locked in on each other. Their lips touched and they kissed passionately. Both of their bodies were on fire as they continued to kiss slowly.

When the kiss was over, Briell sucked on her bottom lip, and Maria moaned softly. She put her hands on his chest and moved her head back and said softly, "Let's go eat."

He kissed her again with a peck to the lips and said, "Ok." They walked to their rooms discussing whether they should order room service or go to the restaurant in the hotel.

"Let's just change and go the to restaurant. We can sit down and eat." Maria suggested.

"That's cool with me. I'm just ready to eat something." Briell shrugged.

"I got something you can eat." Maria mistakenly said aloud.

"What?" Briell said wide-eyed.

"Oh, nothing. I'm just thinking, what if Dillard is in the room with his friend and I walk in." Maria covered.

"If he is, just come to my room and change, and we can go eat from there." Maria knew Dillard wouldn't be in the room with his friend. She just had to say something to throw him off her nasty thoughts. She knew she couldn't be in the room with him right now. Her body was calling for him in the worst way, and she didn't want to take it there with him. She found herself liking Briell, and she knew that wasn't good for business with him having to find love with one of the fifteen chosen women. She didn't want to be a distraction in his decision making.

The two of them walked down the hall to her room. "I'll text you in about 20 minutes. I'm going to take a quick shower and get myself together, and then we can head out." She opened the door quickly and shut it before Briell could say anything. With her back against the door of the suite, she smiled and shook her head. "Get yourself together, Maria."

Briell walked to his room on cloud nine. He was feeling Maria way more than he was supposed to. He tried to shake her out of his mind, but he couldn't. As he showered, he fantasized about the kiss they shared.

Thirty minutes later, she texted him, saying: *"I'm on the way to your room, are you ready?"* He met her in the hallway. When he saw her, his heart fluttered. It was something about Maria that he truly desired. As they got closer, they hugged.

"Damn, this girl smells so good." JaBriell thought.

"Damn, this man feels so good in my arms. I don't want him to let me go." Maria thought as well.

When they reached the restaurant, Maria noticed Angela sitting in a booth with a gentleman. Angela saw the two of them and waved for Maria and Briell to join her and the guy.

Angela looked great to be in her forties. She had a cinnamon complexion, with a short hairstyle like Halle Berry in *"Boomerang."* She was beautiful, with a perfect smile. Her body was toned, and she was thick in the hips and butt. You could tell she worked out. Her clothes and swag were grown and sexy. Her jewelry complemented her beauty. She was classy, and everyone knew it.

She was seated with a guy in his thirties. He was handsome. He pointed to a waitress as soon as Maria and Briell sat down. The waitress came over and asked them what kind of beverages they wanted to drink.

After the waitress took their drink orders, Angela spoke, "Harold, this is Maria and Briell. I hope you don't mind if they join us."

"I don't mind at all." Harold answered.

"They both work with me. JaBriell is whom I was telling you about, he will soon have his own show."

Harold extended his hand to Briell offering him congratulations. "Congratulations, brother."

"Thank you." Briell smiled.

"You two can order whatever you would like to eat. It's on the house." Maria looked at Angela, who winked at her.

"Angela, will you excuse me for one second? I need to handle something." Harold said.

"Sure, Harold, handle your business. We will be here." Angela said politely. Harold smiled and walked away towards the front desk to speak with some customers.

"Damn, Angela, you worked your magic for real." Maria complimented.

"I guess mama still got it." They all laugh as she snapped her finger in the air.

"He's handsome." Maria observed.

"He's also young, and full of fun." Angela added.

"Do I need to be hearing this conversation?" Briell said as they all laughed.

"Yes, you'll learn some game." Angela chuckled. They all laughed again, as the waitress came over with their drinks.

"So where are you two coming from?" Angela asked.

"We were at the jacuzzi. Briell was scared to get in while Dillard was around." Maria revealed.

"No, I wasn't. It wasn't like that. I just didn't feel comfortable, I guess." Briell shrugged.

"Dillard is harmless. He doesn't come on to men that's not in his lane. But I understand. Trust me, you must be careful. You never know what a person's intentions are." She took a sip of her margarita and said, "So where is Dillard now?"

"Some pool guy came in and replaced the towels, and the next thing I knew, after they made eye contact, he left right behind him."

"That must be the guy he was telling me about." Angela shook her head.

"Wait, what? I'm lost. The guy that came in and gave us new towels was coming in there to get Dillard? Man, I didn't see that one." Briell nodded his head in confusion.

"Don't feel bad. It's normal for straight guys to overlook things like this." Angela said taking another sip of her drink "I must say, this is the first business trip that we are all having fun. I've never seen Maria smile so much."

"And I've never seen you get a man sprung so quickly." Maria giggled. Briell looked at Maria causing her to blush as they caught one another's gaze. Angela noticed the chemistry but didn't say anything. Harold returned to the table, and they all ordered food. Forty-minutes later, all their plates were finished, and they were chit-chatting and drinking.

"Maria, can you let Briell entertain you for a bit longer? I'm going to have Harold walk me to my room."

"No problem." Maria agreed. Angela and Harold exit the restaurant and head to the suite.

"You want to watch a movie?" Briell offered.

"Yeah, let's do it." Maria said excitedly. They stood up from the table, and Briell reached in his pocket and left the young waitress a forty-dollar tip.

"That was nice of you." Maria said impressed by the way he carried himself.

"She deserved it, and plus, we got a free meal thanks to Harold." Briell said humbly.

"You're right." They walked onto the elevator with a few people. They were in the back. Briell gently grabbed Maria's hand and held it.

She smiled. When they arrived at his room they walked inside and settled down.

"Have you seen 'Creed 2?'"

"Yeah." Maria answered quickly.

"What about the new 'Mission Impossible?'" Briell said browsing the selections.

"I loves 'Mission Impossible, and I haven't seen the new one. Good pick." Briell chose 'Mission Impossible and the credits began to roll, Maria took off her shoes off laid down in the bed. She settled under the cover. Briell didn't want her to feel uncomfortable, so he got on the bed and laid on top of the covers. Maria loved the fact that he didn't try to have sex with her. That only increased her respect for him. Halfway through the movie, she fell asleep on him. Not long after he ended up falling asleep as well.

CHAPTER 10

At five in the morning Maria's alarm clock went off on her iPhone. She woke up and found Briell's arms around her. He was under the cover with her. She hit the button on her phone and closed her eyes. She felt so good being up under him. He was sound asleep. She moved back to get closer to him and felt his thick, hardened pole between her butt cheeks. His morning wood was turning her on as she grinded slowly on it. She quickly became moist and wet. Her lustful thinking was telling her to let him blow her back out. But her heart made her eyes open and jump up. She took a deep breath as she looked at him.

"Wake up, sleepy head. We got to get ready. You have two hours before we need to be on the set of *'Good Day America.'*"

"Ok, I'm up." Briell said groggily.

She waited a minute, and he didn't move. She woke him up again, and he got up. She kissed him on the cheek and said, "I'm 'bout to go get ready. Don't go back to sleep."

"I'm up." Briell said with a deep stretch.

She left his room and walked down the hall to her suite. Briell soon got up to take a shower. Maria walked in her suite to see Dillard knocked out on the couch. She woke him up and then goes to Angela's room. She wasn't in bed, instead she was in the shower. Maria went to the other bathroom to take a shower, also. By the time she got out, Dillard was waiting for her. As they all hurried to get ready for the talk show, Maria called Briell's phone to make sure he was ready and to inform him they would be heading out in fifteen minutes.

To her surprise, he was ready to go. He was praying and preparing himself for the questions they might ask him. The closer it came to him being on set, the more nervous he became. Fifteen minutes passed and Maria texted him, saying: *Meet us in the lobby. We're heading out now.*

Once in the lobby, Briell saw Maria. She hugged him and asked, "Do you drink coffee?"

"I like hazelnut." He replied.

"I think they have that, come on." Maria led the way to a small coffee shop in the lobby. Once inside the coffee shop the see Dillard who had two cups of coffee in his hands.

"Good morning, Briell. How are you feeling? This is it." Dillard smiled.

Briell takes a deep breath and says, "I'm good. I think this coffee will make me better."

"Don't drink a lot of it if you're not used to drinking coffee. We don't need you having the bubble guts on live television." Maria warned.

"You know what, I'll just take a water and a donut." Briell said on second thought. Maria ordered him a water and donut. Dillard walked over to Angela, who was on the phone. He handed her the other coffee cup as they awaited the town car.

Maria handed Briell his water and donut and said, "Take a deep breath. Everything will be fine, ok?" Briell just nodded his head in agreement. As they walked out the door. The town car pulled up, and Angela and Dillard got inside, followed by Maria and Briell.

"I'll see you in a few." Angela said ending her call.

"Briell, how are you feeling? That was Tracy. She's on the way. Your mom and dad won't make it, but they said they will be watching. When we get there, they will put you in for makeup, which you won't need. They just want to make sure the lighting will be perfect on your face. After that, they'll go over the questions with you. Tracy will be there with you to make sure the questions they ask are appropriate." She briefed him.

A short time later they were arriving at Channel Side where they were filming today's show. They went through security and got cleared for entry. Angela handed Tracy her access badge, and she cleared security before following them to Briell's dressing room.

A woman with a clip board in her hand walked into the dressing room and began to speak, "They'll be ready for you in five minutes."

"Ok." Briell answered after taking a deep breath. Maria walked towards him as he sat in makeup chair, looking at himself in the mirror.

"You can do this. Just stay calm and act natural. Just be yourself. You'll be fine. All of us will be right by the stage if you need us." She looked him in the eye and finished with "You got this."

"We're ready for you." The woman with the clip board announced. They all stood and head out the door.

On stage, Diane and Kristan were closing out their last discussion. Diane looked at the teleprompter and said, "When we return, our next guest is looking for love. Internet sensation JaBriell Gibson is in the house, ladies. Stay tuned." The crowd began to cheer, as the camera men changed positions. A guy held his hand up and counted his fingers down to let them know they were off air.

"Angela, I have to pee." Briell said in a low tone.

"Now?" Angela said looking over at him.

"Yes, now."

"Ok, come on." She rushed him over to the girl with the clip board. "He has to pee. Where's the nearest restroom?" Angela asked abruptly.

"Oh, my God, hurry. This way." She said leading them down the hall.

As he was coming out the restroom, the girl with the clip board screamed, "They're introducing you now. We have to hurry up and get you back up front."

"Welcome back, so ladies, we have a handsome guy by the name of JaBriell Gibson. His friends put him on blast because his girlfriend broke up with him, a video of was made of the moment and has since gone viral. Vanessa Starr aired it on her blog and YouTube channel. After some digging, she found out that not only was JaBriell single, but he was one of the good guys. He has his own business, very family oriented, extremely handsome, and is only twenty-five years old. A bonus is that he has only been with one woman. Vanessa also found out that his ex-broke up with him because she simply needed a break.

They were high school sweethearts. Ladies, I don't know about you, but you don't let someone like this guy get away." Diane spoke.

A picture of JaBriell flashed on the screen, and the ladies in the crowd went wild.

"I know, right? Well, we're not the only ones that think JaBriell is hot. Apparently three million viewers agree, too. Without any further delay, let's bring out JaBriell Gibson." Diane invited. The crowd cheered for him, and he walked out and waved. He was dressed sharp in his chino style fitted *Levi* pants, a fitted Polo purple label shirt, and a pair of *Gucci* loafers on his feet. He left three of his shirt buttons open revealing his gold Cuban link chain and medallion. His sleeves were cuffed revealing his watch and bracelet, also. His smile lit up the room as he sat next to Diane and Kristan.

"Welcome to *'Good Day America.'*" Diane said.

"Thank you, I'm glad to be here." JaBriell smiled.

As the clapping and cheering stopped, Kristan began to speak, "Man, how can I get some of this juice you have. The ladies love you." JaBriell smiled as the ladies screamed and cheered again.

"To break the ice, I heard you had to pee right before we introduced you." Diane laughed a little.

Briell laughed, and Kristan said, "I have to pee right before we start every day. Don't feel bad."

"This is true." Diane reassured him.

"How did you feel when your friend announced that your girl broke up with you and you were newly single?" Diane asked.

"At first I was embarrassed, but the response and the love the ladies began to show me made me feel better." Briell explained.

"I bet a couple lap dances helped also." Kristan added humorously causing everyone to laugh along with her.

"Did you think the blog from Vanessa Starr would reach as many people as it did? I mean, you had the women on *'The View'* discussing you." JaBriell smiled

"Look at that smile, ladies." Diane said with a smile of her own.

"The next day my friend Carlos, barged into my room and said, *"You're blowing up on the Vanessa Starr blog site."* Ironically, he's the same friend who made the announcement at the party. I looked at my phone, and all my social media accounts were blowing up. I was getting a text alert every thirty seconds. It was unbelievable, and when I went to my sandwich shop, the line was almost out the door. So no, I never imagined it would get this big." JaBriell responded.

"Speaking of your sandwich shop, at twenty-five years old you have your own business. That's awesome. We have a few ladies that took selfies of them eating your famous Cuban sandwich. Take a look." Diane said as pictures flooded the screens in the studio. Briell was overwhelmed with joy. He had no idea about the pictures.

"We heard you spent a day with your little sister." Kristan added.

"Yeah, the school year just ended for her, and I know I'll be away from the house for a while because of the reality show, so I decided to spend the day with her. We went shopping and had lunch at Red Lobster. She loved it." JaBriell said coyly.

"I bet she did. We have some of your Instagram pictures you posted." Diane smiled as more pictures flashed. They showed the pics of him and Jassy at the mall with her shopping bags, and then pics of them at Red Lobster. The crowd cheered again.

"Let's get down to the nitty gritty. You just signed on to a reality TV show called 'Finding Love for JaBriell, fifteen women will be fighting for a chance to find love with you." Kristan explained.

"That's going to be a cat fight." Diane commented as everyone laughed.

"How do you feel about that?" Kristan asked.

"It feels good. I'm grateful for the opportunity, but it's also going to be weird because I've never dated or been with any other woman but my ex." JaBriell answered.

"I love you, JaBriell." A woman in the crowd screamed. The crowd was in an uproar as JaBriell just smiled.

"The show will air in three weeks. Everyone make sure that you tune in on *Fox*, Thursday night at eight p.m. I'm sure we will be seeing more of JaBriell Gibson. The ladies love you; we love you, and it was a pleasure meeting you and talking to you. We'll be right back with more 'Good Day America.'" Diane wrapped.

The Director wrapped them up and cut to a commercial, Kristan and Diane shake Briell's hand before he walked off stage.

"Great job, JaBriell. They loved you." Angela cheered shaking his hand.

"Great job, Briell." Dillard said with a pat on the back.

"You were awesome. I told you, that you could do it." Maria said hugging him.

"I'm glad it's over." Briell said breathing a sigh of relief. They walked back to his dressing room and gathered everyone's belongings.

"We're going straight to Clearwater, guys. We will get some food when we get to the villa." Angela announced.

CHAPTER 11

"Ok, guys. Everyone will be here within the next hour. The chef has prepared us a meal, so let's eat and relax a bit, and then it's back to work." Angela announced as they reached the villa. JaBriell grabbed his duffel bag, and suit along with Maria's bag before heading into the villa.

"You're such a gentleman." She smiled.

"This place is bomb, for real. I can't believe I'll be staying here for a month." JaBriell spoke in amazement.

"The inside is just as beautiful." Maria said as they walked inside together.

"Maria, can you show JaBriell what room he will be staying in?" Angela asked.

"Sure. Come on, Briell. You're going to love your room."

"The decor is awesome. I wonder if the paintings on the wall are authentic." JaBriell said taking in the breathtaking scenery in the room.

"That's a good question. I don't know." Maria shrugged.

"No freaking way. This is my room." Briell said with excitement.

Yep, this is all you, Big Baller." Maria said with a pat on the back. His room was huge. He had a sofa and love seat with a coffee table, 50-inch flat screen TV, king size bed decorated with big pillows and a treasure chest at the foot that opened and became a seat. The bathroom had a jacuzzi tub and a walk-in shower with power jet streams.

"I've never been in a shower like this before." He then looks at Maria and said, "Come here."

"What do you want, JaBriell?"

"Just come here, please." He pleaded.

Maria walked inside of the shower with him, and he asked, "Can you imagine taking a shower in here?" He steps closer towards her and grabs her hands and embraces her with a hug and softly kissed her on her neck and whispered in her ear, "Can you imagine making love in here?" Maria smiled as her body became warm from his touch. He kissed her behind her ear. Then moved his tongue slowly down to her neck. Maria was caught up in his spell.

"Yes." She moaned softly answering him.

JaBriell kissed her lips, and her mouth invited him in. They passionately kissed each other, while he ran his hands all over her body. He squeezed her butt, causing her heart to beat faster. Maria tilted her head back submissively, giving in to his pleasure.

"Hey, guys. Lunch is ready." Dillard said interrupting their moment.

Maria pulled away from him and said, "We're looking at the bathroom. Here we come." She smiled at JaBriell and shook her head at him, "You're bad."

"It's your fault." JaBriell smiled back at her.

"How is it my fault?"

"You're in here looking all good, smelling all good, with them sexy-ass lips and body."

"Oh, you think I'm sexy?" Maria asked spinning around to face JaBriell.

"Hell yeah." He agreed. She smiled and kissed his lips before saying, "What am I going to do with you?" She turned around and sashayed her way to the dining area. Briell couldn't keep his eyes off her butt. When they arrived at the dining area and took their seats, Dillard was already at the table looking at his iPhone.

"I know he didn't have that on at the movie premiere." He spoke aloud as he continued to scroll down his timeline.

"Maria, look what Beyonce wore, she slayed it." He said passing the phone to Maria.

"Ok, I'll talk to you later." Angela said as she arrived in the dining area, "We have a long day ahead of us. I need a power nap." She spoke as the chef and a few servers exited the kitchen with food neatly displayed on rolling carts.

The chef announced "We have prepared fresh California sushi rolls, shrimp scampi, grilled flounder, mussels in parmesan sauce, as well as crab cakes. If there are any seafood allergies, we have grilled chicken breast and baked cauliflower. Additionally, we have prepared have a salad with three dressings, Ranch, Caesar, and Thousand Island. Lastly we have an assortment of vegetables." The chef concluded his presentation and stepped to the side.

"Wow, you all have outdone yourselves. This looks amazing." Angela admired.

"Eat as much as you like. We will have food for the entire day. From my understanding there will be a lot more people arriving today."

"Yes, about twenty-five more people."

"Great, there will be plenty." The chef assured.

"I'm going to take a nap. Maria, please make sure I'm up by the time the girls arrive. The camera crew will be here in about forty-five minutes."

"Ok. No problem." Maria answered.

"I'm going to the beach. I'll see you guys in about thirty minutes." Dillard announced.

"It looks like it's just me and you, again." JaBriell smiled.

"You are trouble." Maria said.

"No, you are trouble." They both stood up from the table, "You want to go sit on the beach, or you want to chill inside?"

"I really just want to relax before the guests arrive, your guests." Maria interated.

"The shade you throw." JaBriell smirked.

"It's not shade, it's the truth." They returned to Briell's room, and she sat on the bed "I'm about to lay down. Don't come over here bothering me."

"This is my room and my bed, and the most beautiful woman is laying in it, and she says I can't bother her." Briell said turning on the television. He jumped on the bed and started play fighting with her. Maria screamed and laughed as he pinned her down kissing her. Suddenly she flipped him over, and now she's on top of him.

"You didn't think I was that strong, huh?" Maria asked with a smile.

"Naw, but I kind of like it when you're rough." Briell licked his lips.

"What else do you like?" Maria asked. JaBriell grabbed her butt with both of his hands and pulls her down on his manhood. She began to grind on it slowly, as it grew harder. She moved his hands from her butt and placed them over his head before kissing him. She then stood up and walked away from the job.

"I told you, don't bother me." She then laid on the love seat.

'That's how you gone play it." Briell asked looking at her.

"Yep."

"Ok, I'll be good. Come back to the bed." He asked.

"That smile is what got me in this predicament. I'm not coming." Maria declined.

"Please." He groveled.

"Are you going to be good?"

"Yes, I'll be good." He complied. Maria moved from the love seat back to the bed with him.

"I'm not supposed to like you, JaBriell." She confessed.

"I like you, too." JaBriell returned. He kissed her on the neck, and they relaxed in each other's arms. An hour later, her phone rang. She answered in a groggy tone.

"Hello?"

"Yes, Mrs. Vasquez, Mrs. Angela Curtis gave me your number as an alternate if I could not reach her. I'm Henry with Spotlight Productions. We just arrived at the villa. Can someone let us in to get everything set up?"

"Yes. My apologies, we had an early morning. I'm coming now."

"Is everything ok?" Briell asked woken from his sleep.

"Yeah, the camera people are here. I have to let them in to get set up." Maria said in a hurry.

"Should I get up, too?" Briell asked.

"No, no, get some rest. I'll come get you when your girls arrive." Maria said kissing him.

"Not funny."

"Mmmhhh..." she said as she walked out the door. When Maria arrived downstairs, she allowed Henry and his crew in.

"How long have they been here?" Dillard asked walking out of his room.

"They just arrived. I'm going to change my clothes and get ready. I know the girls will be here shortly." Maria said.

Suddenly there was a knock at the door. Maria looked at Dillard. "I hope that's not them arriving already."

"It shouldn't be. They're not scheduled to arrive for another hour." Dillard replied. Maria opened the door, and two girls with bags stood in front of her.

"Hi, I'm Racheal, and this is Candy. We're the makeup artists." One of the girls announced.

"Oh, yeah. Come on in, girls." Maria invited.

"Wow, this place is to die for." Rachel admired.

"Girl, this is amazing." Candy agreed.

"It sure is. We have a spot for you all to set up. It has mirrors and plenty of light." Maria said before showing them to the spot where they would be working.

"Take your time and set up. The camera people just got here as well. There's food and drinks in the dining room if y'all want something to eat before you get started." Maria invited.

"Thank you." The two women said sitting there bags down.

"No problem. I'm going to get ready, I'll let you all get to it." Maria turned on her heels and walked away.

"Ok, I'll have them set up. I'm going to get ready. It's all on you now." Maria said to Dillard.

"Hurry up, I have to get ready too." Dillard whined. Maria turned and made her way to the room where she began to get ready. Thirty minutes passed and she emerged from her room looking stunning in a pair of tight Christian Dior pants and a DKNY blouse, with sleek pair of Jimmy Choo shoes on her feet. Candy pressed her long hair, that hung down her back. Racheal put a light coat of foundation on her face and eyeliner on her eyes. She looked like the star of the show. When she was through she noticed a few girls began to arrive and went to wake Angela up.

"Girl, I've never seen you this dolled up before. You're slaying those pants." Angela squealed as she looked Maria over.

"Let me get ready. I'll see you in a minute." Angela said disappearing into the bathroom.

"Okay and thank you." Maria smiled. Maria went to show the girls where Racheal and Candy were.

"O.M. fucking G. Girl, you look fabulous. Let me look at you." Dillard exclaimed as he spotted Maria. Maria spun around on her heels. "Girl, you got too much booty in them pants." He said as he playfully smacked her butt.

"I'll assist the girls in signing in, can you wake JaBriell up and tell him we're doing the suit scene first?" Maria requested.

"I got you." Dillard threw her the thumbs up. Dillard went to wake Briell up and relayed the message regarding the suit. When JaBriell walked down the stairs he was greeted by the ladies who were all dressed in beautiful dresses and heels. Their makeup was flawless, as was their hair. Although the women were beautiful, his eyes scanned the room for Maria. He politely smiled and introduced himself to everyone. Shortly thereafter Angela and Maria appeared in the room. When JaBriell saw Maria, time seemed to move in slow motion. She moved her hair from her face, leaving JaBriell stunned. Her beauty put him in a trance. He looked at the girls, then back to her, and there was no comparison. She was the most gorgeous woman in the room.

"Hello, everyone." Angela greeted stepping forward.

"Hey," the girls spoke in unison.

"Ladies, this is JaBriell Gibson. You all will be competing for an opportunity to find love. The cameras will be rolling shortly, I want you to introduce yourselves, with your name and where you're from, also tell him why you're the one. Is everyone ready?" Angela asked with her hands extended to the girls.

"Henry, it's all yours. Let's help JaBriell find love, shall we?" Angela said as she moved to the side.

JaBriell couldn't help but look at Maria. They stared at each other for a moment, their intense gaze was broken when one of the producers holding up a sign walked forward and yelled "Scene one, take one."

"Action." Henry screamed, the first young lady moved forward on cue and introduced herself.

"Hi, I'm Ayanna, and I'm from Sarasota, Florida, and I'm looking forward to spending my time in Clearwater with you, JaBriell." She moved back to the line and allowed the next contender to move forward.

"Hi, I'm Crystal, and I'm from Lakeland, Florida, and JaBriell, you won't go wrong with me in your corner." She said sweetly.

"Hi, I'm Amber, I'm from Tampa, Florida and JaBriell, you're looking at your future wife." She said placing her hand on her hips and accentuating her curves. Maria was not at all impressed. Although she was in her feelings, she was trying her hardest not to show it.

"Hi, I'm Marissa, and I'm from St. Petersburg, Florida. JaBriell, I'm all you need." She said winking her eye at him as she stepped back in line.

"Hi, I'm Sandra, and I'm from Tampa, we're from the same place, so you know we are meant to be." The next woman spoke with confidence. Ten other girls followed the same routine, giving their names and a brief introduction. After an hour the first part of the commercial was done. They filmed two additional scenes; one was a makeshift date and the next was a pool scene. When filming wrapped everyone sat down to talk and eat

"Good job today, guys. I am taking an Uber back to the hotel. I have a date. Our flight leaves in two days, we have a full day left in Tampa until we return in two weeks for the start of the show."

"I want to go back now, too. My friend is waiting for me." Dillard said.

"You two go ahead. I'll make sure everything is done here. Me and Briell will take the town car back." Maria spoke up.

"Ok, cool. Call me if you need me." Angela said proud that Maria was willing to take the lead. The three of them hugged and Dillard and Angela went to gather their things.

By nine-thirty everyone had left the villa. The only people left were the cleaning crew. It didn't take long for them to wrap up also. An older lady approached Maria while her and Briell were on the couch. "Mrs. Vasquez, everything is done. We are leaving now."

"Thank you so much." Maria said with a smile.

"No problem at all. Your husband is very handsome." The woman winked at Maria.

"What did she say?" Briell asked with his ears perked up.

"She said that my husband, you, were very handsome." Maria smiled.

"Isn't that sweet? Even old ladies think I'm handsome." Briell joked as they both laughed. He stood up and locked the front door before going into the kitchen.

"Wifey, do you want something to drink?" Briell called from the kitchen.

"Alcohol, please." Maria called back to him.

Briell prepared drinks made with pineapple juice and vodka, and then returned to the living room. "We have this villa all to ourselves. What are we going to do?" Briell asked as he handed Maria her drink.

"Are you trying to get me drunk?" Maria joked.

"Yep." Briell laughed.

"You are too much." Maria said tossing a pillow in Briell's direction. The two of them sat on the couch and talked for hours about everything from childhood, life goals, relationships, celebrities, and more. After four drinks, the two of them were very tipsy.

"I can't cap, you were the baddest girl in the villa today. I swear when I saw you, I wanted to run into your arms and kiss you. You had me shook, real talk." Briell admitted.

"Well, I can't cap, I did that on purpose. I wanted you to see me glammed up. Angela and Dillard never saw me like that before, either. They were surprised. I'm tipsy. I'm going to take a quick shower. I'll meet you in the room, ok?"

"I'll be waiting." Briell said watching as she walked away, "Whoop, whoop, pull over, that ass too fat." Maria laughed began to twerk a little. Briell started laughing as she walked away. He followed suit walking to his room to take a shower also.

After his shower, he sat on the edge of the bed flipping through the channels. Maria walked into wearing a sexy pink lace bra and panty set. Briell's mouth fell open and he dropped the remote. He quickly picked it up as he struggled to regain his composure. Maria slowly walked up to him and grabbed the remote out of his hand and turned the television off. She grabbed his head and slowly pushed his face to her stomach. He kissed her gently, as she held his head and rubbed his hair.

JaBriell picked her up and placed her on the bed. He climbed on top of her and kissed her neck, making a trail down to her breast. He slowly removed her bra and sucked on her breast while flickering his tongue on along her nipple. He then moved to the other one. As he continued to suck on her breast, his finger rubbed between her legs. Maria was moaning with pleasure. He made his way down her navel and kissed her flesh. He pulled off her panties, as his tongue moved slowly down to her box. Briell puts his tongue on her clit and licked her slowly. He began sucking on her clit slow and sensually.

"Yes, like that." Maria yelled gasping for air. He continued to please her, while she moaned and pulled his hair. After she climaxed, he continued to kiss her neck. Maria pulled off his boxers off, guided him inside her. The two of them made love all night. When they finally finished, they held each other closely.

Morning came quickly, as soon as the two of them awoke they made love again and then fell back asleep. When Maria woke up, she went to take a shower. As the warm water hit her body, she felt Briell's hands wrap around her waist. She smiled and turned around, and they began to kiss, and make love in the shower.

When they were through, she put on a new bra and panty set along with her robe and made her way into the kitchen. Maria cooked breakfast for the two of them while humming love songs. Briell was impressed at the sight of her in the kitchen.

"Wow, and she cooks too." He commented as he took a seat at the kitchen table.

"My mom taught me how to cook. Breakfast food is easy. Except grits, you must be careful how much water you put in them. I hate really runny grits." She handed him a plate with turkey bacon, eggs, fried potatoes, and cheese grits.

"Damn, you can cook." JaBriell complimented with a mouthful of food.

"Thank you." She smiled. Maria took a seat beside him at the kitchen table. Together they ate and talked for hours. Their conversation was genuine, there was never an awkward or dull moment. Shortly afterward the two of them changed clothes and laid on the beach together. They played in the ocean, and even rented jet skis and rode over the ocean waves. Maria and JaBriell spent the whole day enjoying one another's company. Before the day ended and they returned to Tampa they made love one last time.

"I hate that you'll be gone for two whole weeks. Do you think you can come back sooner?" JaBriell asked stroking Maria's hair.

"I doubt it, but I will be back." Maria said reassuringly.

"I'm going go to home tonight, so you can work in peace. I'm sure you and Angela has things to discuss in reference to the show." He informed her.

"Yeah, we do. It's going to be crazy when we get back to New York. There is a lot of work to be done." Maria added.

"I'm doing this show because I have to, but I want you, Maria. I want to be with you. I care about you a lot."

"I care about you, too. I've never felt this close to anyone. It's like we were made for each other." Maria admitted.

"I will choose someone, but that's where it will end, so that you and I can be together. You said it yourself, if two people loved each other, they would make their relationship work regardless of where they are in the world or what they do for a living."

"You love me, JaBriell?" Maria asked with tears filling her eyes.

"I know it sounds crazy, but I think I do. No, I know I do. When we're together, it feels right. I never felt this way with my ex. This isn't a rebound, this is real. The feelings I have for you are real."

"I feel the same way about you. I want to be with you, too. I've fallen for you." Maria admitted with tears streaming down her face.

"As soon as the show is done filming, we can be together. I don't want to hide you, or my feelings for you." JaBriell replied. Maria looked up and noticed Dillard walking over to the table. She quickly moved her hand from Briell's hand and wipes her tears away. She straightened her posture and put on a smile.

"What's up, Dillard? What you got going on?" she spoke cheerfully.

"Girl, nothing. I Just went to say goodbye to my friend. I can't wait to see him again. Anyway, what did you'll order? I'm starving." Dilliard replied.

"Nothing for you. Go ahead and order yourself something." Maria said with a chuckle.

"I wish I could order my friend to get on the plane with us to New York." Dilliard and Maria began to laugh while Briell shook his head in disbelief at the conversation.

"Oh, Lord." Briell commented, still reeling from Dilliard's comment. The waitress soon arrived at the table with their plates and they each dug in quickly.

Once they were finished eating Briell ordered an Uber and prepared to leave. "Well guys, my Uber will be here in a minute." He announced standing up from the table. He picked up his bags and then shook Dilliard's hand.

"See you in a couple weeks, Tell Angela I'll see her soon."

"I'll walk you out." Maria said as he turned to her.

The two of them walked outside together as the Uber arrived. They shared a tight hug. "I'll see you in two weeks. I love you." JaBriell said looking her in the eyes.

"I love you, too. See you soon." Maria offered a coy smile.

"I'll text you later." JaBriell said as he walked towards the car.

"Ok." She agreed. As his car took off in the direction of home.

CHAPTER 12

A few days passed and Maria was back in New York setting up the conference room for the meeting. The commercial was finally edited, and the team was preparing to view it for the first time. They only had two days to make any necessary changes before it aired.

Dillard walked in with a box of bagels and orange juice. He placed the box and the orange juice on a small table before turning on his heels quickly. "I'll be right back. I have to get the cups and paper plates out of the break room."

"Ok. Don't forget the napkins." Maria called out behind him.

She continued setting up for the meeting as members of the team began filling the room. Dillard returned with the plates, cups, and napkins. Everyone took their respective seats and patiently awaited Angela and the CEO, Mr. Hopkins. The two of them arrived shortly thereafter. Maria began the meeting with opening remarks. She gave minutes and read over the reports. The group then engaged in viewing the commercial. They were all pleased with the outcome.

The CEO of the company offered Angela congratulations on a job well done. He also gave a compliment to Maria for all her hard work. He informed her he would like to see her in his office and then exited the conference room.

Maria straightened up the conference room and then headed to Mr. Hopkins's office. She informed his secretary that she was there to see him and then took a seat on the couch

"Mr. Hopkins will see you now." The secretary said.

Maria stood up from the sofa a bit nervous. She'd never been in Mr. Hopkins's office before, and she was curious about what he wanted to discuss with her.

"Mrs. Vasquez, how are you? That was a great presentation you did this morning." He greeted her as she walked through the doors.

"Thank you." She smiled taking a seat in front of him.

"You're quite welcome. I wanted to discuss some things with you in private. I never get into any of my employees' personal business, especially who they date, but this thing you have going on with Mr. Gibson is bad for business. You can't return to Florida for filming. I don't want your personal relationship to interfere with his decisions on choosing someone for this show. I hear you two became really close during your last visit. If he weren't the star of the show, I wouldn't care as much. However, we need him to focus on the women that you all picked for him." He paused for a minute.

"If you are present, his judgment may be clouded. More importantly you may get hurt. Angela and I have plans for you at this company. We both think highly of you. Before your relationship with Mr. Gibson blows up, we need to just nip it in the bud. I'm not criticizing you for falling in love. I'm also not taking your position from you. I'm going to give you a promotion. I want you to be the new head of marketing. It's a pay raise, but you won't be in the field any longer. You will be going out of town with your own team, handling marketing for all the current and new shows, except *"Finding Love for JaBriell."* That would be considered a conflict of interest. I'll give you to the end of the day to let me know your decision. That will be all, thank you."

"Thank you, sir." Maria stood and walked out of the office broken hearted. When she reached the elevator tears began streaming down her face. She had finally found true love, and more importantly someone who loved her, too. Maria found a good man in JaBriell. When the elevator stopped, she exited and slightly began to run towards the women's restroom. She didn't want anyone seeing her crying. The more she wiped away her tears, the more they flowed.

The door of the restroom opened slowly, and Angela walked inside, when she saw Maria crying, she locked the door behind her. Angela connected to Maria's hurt immediately. She knew the pain she felt all too well. Angela opened her arms wide to Maria and Maria fell into her chest crying hard.

"Let it out, baby. It's going to be okay." By the way Maria was crying, she knew that she truly loved Briell, this made Angela sad for her.

"I finally found someone that loved me for me, and we can't be together. Now I have to choose him or my job." Maria spoke through tears.

"I had no idea what was going on with you and JaBriell. I was shocked when Mr. Hopkins told me what Dillard revealed to him when we were on the way to the meeting. He even told me that I shouldn't have allowed you two to become so close. Honestly, I suspected that you two liked each other, but I never imagined it was this deep. You're like a daughter to me, Maria. I want you to be happy and find love. You deserve it, you work so hard. I would never get in the way of that, but these men see things different. They can sleep with coworkers, women of the show, and they give each other high fives about it. When it comes to us women, we can't conduct ourselves in that manner. It's not good for business. I'm glad the mask fell off Dillard's fake face. I know I can't do anything in front of him. This is a lesson for both of us."

Angela wiped Maria's face with her hand and then held her chin up, "Listen to me. Take this new position, and the pay raise, learn everything there is to know about marketing, and in a year if you want to leave the company, I'll recommend you to another company. If it's meant to between you and JaBriell, you all will be together. Keep your faith. I love you, girl. Now get yourself together, you have a whole department to run. Hell, you'll be my boss before it's all over with." Angela laughed as the two of them shared an embrace.

"Thank you, girl. I needed that pep talk." Maria said wiping the remaining tears from her eyes.

"Anytime you need me, I'll be here for you, just like you have been there for me." Angela returned. They hugged again and left the bathroom together. When they came out, a woman was there pacing back and forth. When she saw them come out, she says, "Why would you lock the door? I'm about to pee on myself." She said as she rushed past them. Angela and Maria looked at each other and burst out laughing.

"I'm 'bout to pee on myself." Angela said mocking the woman's voice. They laughed again.

"Girl, you are crazy." Maria giggled.

CHAPTER 13

JaBriell, Thadd, and Squirt were walking away from the basketball court. They had just finished playing a team, and they lost.

Squirt says, "Briell, what's going on with you, bro? You ain't have no hustle, and you ain't make no buckets. Your game was all the way off today. How you let Thadd outscore you?" JaBriell just sat on the bench, looking sad.

"What's on your mind, man? Ever since earlier this week you haven't been yourself." Thadd asked.

"Yeah, man. You got all this good stuff going on in your life, and you sitting around looking like you lost your best friend. We're your boys, man. What's good? Something happened with the show?" Squirt chimed in.

"I was going to wait until after the show to tell you'll this. Remember when I left y'all at the strip club that night?" Briell asked leading into his story.

"Yeah." Thadd and squirt said in unison.

"Well, when I left, I took Maria some food."

"You mean big booty." Squirt joked.

"The bad Spanish chick." Thadd added.

"Yeah. Well, after that we started texting each other, talking all the time. Se spent the noht with me in my hotel room the night before *Good Day America*. The day after the commercial shoot, we stayed the night at the villa and afterwards spent the whole day together. We connected on a level me and Vonne have never been on. It was deeper than sex. Man, I messed around and fell in love with this girl. I know it sounds crazy, but it's true. I don't know, maybe I needed something after Vonne, and maybe she needed something special in her life. She told me she hadn't been with anyone since college, and she got her degree three years ago." Briell paused taking I n his own thoughts.

"We made plans to be together after the show airs. I was just going to pick someone and act like I liked them. When I was leaving the hotel, we told each other I love you. I believed her. Hell, she had tears in her eyes. Then a couple days ago she tells me that we can't be together and that she's not coming back to Tampa to do the show. She said it would be bad for business. I've been hurt ever since, man. I'm so confused. Like how can God send the perfect girl for me in my life and then take her out my life? I just don't get it. She was so different, bro. Like for real I wanted to marry this girl." He finished dropping his head.

"I'm sorry, man. I had no idea. Just give her time, maybe things just happened too fast for her. If she's the one and you feel that God put her in your life for a reason, don't give up on her. Just be patient. It must be a reason she froze up like that." Thadd reasoned.

"Yeah, the reason is y'all both used each other for pleasure purposes and the sparks were flying, and now the flame is gone, and reality sunk in. You're in Tampa, and she's in New York. You have a show that starts filming next week. You have fifteen women competing for your attention. Bro, you have to play your cards right with this show. Who knows, you might get another show after this one. The women love you. Your buzz is getting bigger and bigger every day. Who knows what God has planned for you? Do you know how many brothers would love to be in your position right now? This platform can be used for you to do so many other things, even help young males. Keep your head up. I do agree with Thadd. If she's the one God sent for you, y'all will be together. Just give it time." Squirt advised.

"'Preciate it, bro. I needed to hear that." JaBriell said as Squirt held out his hand and gav e him some dap.

"So, since that's out the way, can I please tell y'all my story?" Thadd quickly said.

"What's up, Thaddy Thadd? What's on your mind?" Squirt asked comically.

"Remember the girls at the party that took pics of me while I was drunk and asleep?" Thadd asked leading into his story.

"Yeah." Briell and Squirt said in unison.

"Well, we've been kicking it on Facebook, and the other night I invited them to my crib to eat some crab legs and drink. After we ate, we continued to drink, then we took shots, and then after that," Thadd paused for dramatic effect.

"Spit it out, Bro." Squirt yelled.

"I smashed both of them." Thadd confessed with a deep sigh of relief.

"What! Get the fuck out of here" Briell exclaimed.

"No cap, bro. Real talk." Thadd help up his hands in sincerity.

"How did this man have a threesome before me?" Squirt wondered aloud. The three of them laughed and then Briell and Squirt gave Thadd some dap. As they walked away from the bench, Squirt started singing Future's song "I Fucked Two Bad Sisters"

"At the same damn time." The three of them sang in harmony.

CHAPTER 14

Today was the day. Briell's bags were packed, and he was waiting for the town car to pick him up. He was on his way to Clearwater Tampa. He walked downstairs and saw his dad.

"I'm proud of you, son." Jamal said as they hugged and then shook hands. Stephanie walked out of the kitchen with Jassy. When Briell saw his sister, she was crying.

"What's wrong, Jassy?" Briell asked concerned about his little sister.

"You're leaving me, again." She cried.

"I'm not leaving you, Jassy. I'm going to do the show so I can be on T.V. I just have to be there for a month, and then I'll be back."

"You better come back." She demanded running from behind her mom and punching him in the stomach. Stephanie and Jamaal laughed, before the four of them shared a hug. The doorbell ringing disrupted their moment. Jamal walked over to answer it.

"Good afternoon. I'm here to pick up Mr. JaBriell Gibson." The driver announced.

"That's me. I'm ready." Briell responded.

"May I have your bags, sir?" The driver asked politely. Jamal handed the driver Briell's bags while he hugged his mother and sister. After that, he hugged his father, and then entered the town car. On the ride to Clearwater, he thought about Maria. He missed her, but he had to do what he needed to do for him, and that was film this show. When he arrived at the villa, he went into his room and unpacked. Once he was done, he sat on the edge of the bed and thought about Maria again.

Angela walked in his room. She saw that he was in deep thought, so she knocked on the door while standing in the doorway.

"Hey, Mrs. Angela, how are you?" JaBriell said looking up and offering her a half smile.

"I'm fine, but the question is, how are you doing?"

Briell took a deep breath and shook his head from left and right. Angela proceeded to walk into the room and take a seat beside him on the bed. "I miss her so much. I don't understand what I did." Briell confessed with watery eyes.

In that moment Angela realized JaBriell loved Maria just as much as she loved him. "JaBriell, you didn't do anything. Sometimes true love takes time. You have to be patient, have faith, and most importantly don't give up on Maria. Believe me, she loves you." Angela encouraged.

"You know, my homeboy told me to be patient and have faith too." Briell informed her.

"Well, he gave you some good advice."

"I'm trying to be patient, and I'm trying to understand the whole situation. When two people love each other, they stay together. So why can't me and Maria be together?"

"Keep your faith, Baby. Everything will work out in due time. Always remember God has a plan for you and Maria."

"Thank you, Angela."

"No problem. And if you ever need to talk, I'm right here. Don't be afraid to come to me. I made a promise to your mom that I would make sure you were good, and I don't want to get on her bad side." They shared a laugh, before Angela spoke again, "I knew that pretty smile would surface soon."

"Moving forward, you are the star of this show, and it must go on. Stop looking sad and receive this blessing. Come on, get up. The chef made some barbecue chicken. I know you like barbecue."

"Yes, I do." He agreed, standing up from the side of the bed.

"Good, now put some swag in your step. Let them know who got the juice." She cheered him on. The two of them exited the room and JaBriell walked out with a swag step and bop in his walk.

"Yeah, that's it. Who got the juice?" Angela asked egging him on even more.

"I do." Briell answered in a confident tone.

"Who got the juice?" Angela asked again.

"I do." Briell said with even more confidence as he began walking like George Jefferson. Angela laughed and then started mocking his walk.

"I got juice too." She said as the two of them headed to the dining room. The camera filmed them unknowingly. Their act made both the girls and the camera crew laugh hysterically.

"You feel better now? Are you ready to get your blessing?" Angela asked in a low tone as they settled in the kitchen.

"Yeah." Briell said with much confidence.

"That's what I want to hear." Angela smiled before looking at the chef and his crew. "Chef, the star of the show would like some barbecue chicken."

"A nice big plate, chef." Briell added.

"Coming right up." Chef nodded.

I'll see you later. I got some other work to do." Angela said still in character from earlier. He smiled and laughed at her as she walked out of the kitchen, walking like George Jefferson.

"Thank you, Lord." Angela whispered as she exited the kitchen.

CHAPTER 15

Two weeks had passed since filming began. JaBriell had ten ladies left, and tonight there would be another round of eliminations. He was out on a date with Jessica. They were on a boat relaxing and eating lunch. He enjoyed Jessica's company. She was one of the girls he liked. She was a light brown skin chick from Pensacola, Florida. She had long hair, light brown eyes, and a body like a stripper. Briell couldn't believe how big her butt was. He wondered if it was real or not. He admired how good she looked in the two-piece bikini she was wearing. She had on a big sun hat on with a pair of *Gucci* sunglasses. Briell liked that he could hold a good conversation with her.

After they ate, they were both laying on a set of lawn chairs enjoying the view of the ocean. "How do you feel about tonight? Have you decided on who you're going to send home?" She asked breaking the silence between them.

"Yep, it's going to be you." Briell joked, smiling at her.

"Don't be scaring me like that." She smiled in return.

"Naw, I'm not going to send you home. I like you."

"Oh, you like me." She responded in a sexy tone. She stood up out of her chair and straddled Briell, before kissing him. He kissed her back. The rest of their date consisted of kissing and cuddling with one another.

His second date was with Joi. He was digging Joi, too. Their date was at an art painting lesson. They painted a picture together. After painting, they sat at a table drinking champagne with strawberries in the glasses. They shared a deep conversation about love. While Joi sipped her flute glass, she waited patiently for Briell to answer her question.

"I thought I felt love, but I don't think it was real." He took out his phone and went to his pictures. He comes to a picture of his parents. He shows Joi the picture and says, "This is the type of love I want to feel. My parents have been together since high school. My mom had me when she was seventeen years old. My dad had scholarship opportunities to go to several colleges or football. He chose to go to USF to be with my mom and me. They received their degrees at USF, they married shortly after. They have been together since. Seven years ago, they had my little sister Jasmine." He showed Joi a picture of Jasmine, and then he said, "It seems as if they are more in love now than ever. That's the type of love I want, that's the type of love I want to feel."

"I feel you, and the way you just broke it down I feel like I never felt love, but I want to." Joi confessed.

"A wise and special person told me to have faith and be patient, and that's something I feel every person looking for love or anything should do." They continued to converse about things, until the date came to an end.

The two dates were totally different. The one with Jessica was more intimate than the one with Joi. He was pleased with both. He began to think about Maria. Maria was like Jessica and Joi, all in one. With Maria he had the intimacy and good conversation. Even though he wasn't intimate with Joi, he had feelings for her because she had good conversation. Tonight, he had to eliminate five women. Jessica and Joi were staying in the villa for sure.

For the past couple Thursdays, social media fans were weighing in on whom they thought JaBriell should be with, and who should be eliminated. They commented on which girls seemed thirsty, or lame. Fans even created a hashtag #whoshouldbrielltakehometomama.

The time for eliminations had come, and JaBriell was standing in front of the remaining ten women. It was time for him to let the world and the ladies know who would stay and who would go.

"The first person I'm sending home tonight is Nikki. I think you're beautiful and have so much potential to find a good man, we just didn't share the connection I was looking for.

"The second person is Brittany. We shared a vibe on a good friend level. I feel like after the show we could still have a friendship.

"The third lady to be eliminated is Michelle." Before he could say anything else, Sandra starts to snicker loudly before saying "Ha! Ha." Michelle looked at her, and Sandra waved her hand.

"Bye, Bitch. Hit the road, Jack." Sandra went on.

"Who're you calling a bitch, Bitch?" The show was live, so they were unable bleep out what they said.

"You. You're the one I'm talking to." Sandra said boldly. Michelle and Sandra had been beefing for the past few weeks in the villa. They had two or three arguments and almost got into a fight, but security broke it up. Michelle walked up towards Sandra and the other girls around Sandra moved out the way.

"I'm tired of your disrespectful-ass mouth. If I'm leaving, I'm leaving with a bang." She proceeded to punch Sandra in the mouth. Sandra caught her balance and swung back and hitting Michelle. Michelle grabbed Sandra's hair and started swinging wildly. They both fell on the ground, and as they continued to fight, security came and broke them up.

It happened so fast that the full fight was aired on the show before they could go to commercial. Once the show came from commercial break, Briell was standing in front of the remaining girls. He sent two more home, additionally Sandra was sent home due to her behavior.

Jessica, Joi, Marissa, and Kendra were in the villa with Briell. They were at the bar drinking and talking about the fight with Michelle and Sandra. Briell decided it was time for bed, leaving the girls to chat he walked to his room. He took a shower in effort to sober up a bit. The shower was unsuccessful in washing away his tipsiness. Briell turned the lights off and climbed in bed.

Forty minutes passed and Jessica walked into his room. She got in the bed and started kissing on him. She then climbed on top of him. "I want you." She moaned softly. As she continued to kiss his neck and rub on his manhood.

"I want to feel him." She said as she began grind on Briell, the show came to an end, leaving the viewers to wonder what happened.

CHAPTER 16

Back In New York

One week later, Maria was walking into the building at High Rise Productions. She was running late. She had been feeling under the weather the last few days. As she got off the elevator, and her coworkers were running around working. "What's going on? Why is everyone so turned up?" She asked Cindy.

"You don't know?" Cindy replied quickly.

"Really, Cindy, if I would have known I would not have asked you." Maria said with an eye roll.

"'*Finding Love for JaBriell*' broke rating records. Last week's episode made it the number one show on the network. The fight between those two girls has gone viral. They even have memes of the fight on Instagram and Facebook. They're hilarious." Maria was in shock. She had been so caught up with her own work she didn't even look at the show.

"The big question on Twitter about last week's episode is did JaBriell have sex with Jessica." Cindy added.

"Did he have sex with her?" Maria's heart began to beat fast as she took in the news.

"We don't know. The production crew down there knows, though." she added. Maria walked away off from Cindy without saying anything else. She walked into the women's restroom and ran to the toilet. She threw up, almost immediately. She was heartbroken. Just hearing about Briell and some other woman having sex hurt her to the core. After she threw up, she walked over to the sink to clean herself up. Tears were streaming down her face as her thoughts raced. She picked up her phone and hit contacts. The phone began to ring her ear, on the last ring before the voicemail Angela answered.

"Hello?"

"Hi, Angela." Maria said gathering some strength into her voice.

"Maria, hey Baby, how are you? What's up?"

"Oh, nothing. Just found out the great news about the show being number one and breaking records."

"Yes, girl. These women are going crazy over JaBriell." She exclaimed. Maria became quiet. She was angry and hurt. She was angry because she left him and hurt because he was being romantic and intimate with other women.

"Maria, you still there?" Angela said confused by the awkward silence.

"Yeah, Um, Angela, did he have sex with that woman?" Maria blurted out.

"Maria, he turned her down. They didn't have sex. JaBriell is a good man." Angela assured her.

Maria took a deep breath and said, with tears in her eyes, "I know he is."

"Do you want talk to him? I'm pretty sure he would love to hear your voice."

"Maybe I'll call him later. I'm just getting to the office, it's crazy here. Can you keep our conversation between us?" Angela knew she didn't want JaBriell knowing she called to check on him, especially what he was doing with other women.

"I got you, girl."

"Thank you. Talk to you soon." Maria said as they hang up. Maria looked herself in the mirror and straightened her clothes, and then ran her hands through her hair before leaving the bathroom.

Before she could get to her office, Bryan said, "Hey, Maria, Mr. Hopkins needs to see you in his office."

"Ok. Thanks, Bryan." She said heading to Mr. Hopkins's office.

"He's waiting for you. You can go right in." his secretary said.

Good morning, Mr. Hopkins. You wanted to see me?"

"Yes, Maria. Come in, come in. Have a seat." She sat down, and he began speaking again, "I know you've probably heard that *Finding Love for JaBriell' is the number one show."*

"Yes, I'm aware."

"Good. Next week will be the finale. I need you and your team down in Clearwater. I need two new commercials, and I need them hot. I want the viewers to have something to look forward to. You're my chief marketing and design director, and I need you to make it happen. This thing with you and JaBriell won't be a problem, will it?"

"No, sir. It won't."

"Good. Get the team together, and head down there to get all the footage you need to make it happen. This kid might get another show. He's on fire right now." Mr. Hopkins beamed.

"I'm on it, sir." Maria said as she walked out of his office and got onto the elevator. "Oh, now I can go back to Clearwater." She spoke aloud to herself.

CHAPTER 17

I t was Tuesday morning, JaBriell got up and went to look for Angela. He called her and asked if they could meet out on the patio. Twenty minutes later, Briell and Angela were having breakfast out on the patio.

"Angela, I want to have a little kick back Thursday. Just a few people, of course. I'll have my best friends Squirt and Thadd here. I want to unwind before next week's final decision, and I want Squirt and Thadd to talk to the girls one by one to see what they think. Their opinion matters to me."

"Honestly, that's never been done on a show like this, but I don't see anything wrong with it, I guess." Angela nodded taking in the idea.

"I want the ratings to remain high and being different can be a good thing sometimes. Trust me, it will be fine." Angela reassured him. "Ok, Briell. Let's do it. Do I need to do anything on my end to make the kick back a success?"

"Just make sure we have plenty of liquor and food." Briell informed her.

"Ok. And one more thing, what exactly is a kick back?" Angela asked.

"Of course. It's a little party, where you can relax. You know, kick back." Briell chuckled.

"Okay." she nodded her head again as they finished their breakfast.

"Have you spoken with Maria? How has she been?" Briell asked suddenly.

"Ummm, I haven't spoken to her, but I'm pretty sure she's doing fine. Have you tried to call her?" Angela lied.

"I'm pretty sure she doesn't want to talk to me, Angela. If she did, she would have Angela hated to be in the middle of JaBriell and Maria's mess. She knew they both loved each other and missed one another, but she told Maria that she wouldn't let JaBriell know they had been talking.

"I didn't sleep with Jessica." He called out behind Angela.

"I know, JaBriell." Angela smiled.

"I really love Maria, and I'm not a thirsty guy that needs to sleep with a woman because she throws herself at me. I'm only engaging as far as kissing and touching because I know it's good for T.V. And if I make it good for TV, then it's good for you. And if it's good for you, then it's good for me, everybody's happy." Briell reasoned.

"I see you have this good-for-business thing down pack, but let me ask you this, and you ask yourself, all of this, is it good for you and Maria?" After she said that, she walked away without getting a response from Briell. He sat there on the patio thinking about Angela's last comment.

Later that day, JaBriell went on a date with Marissa and then a date with Kendra. He wanted to get all his dates out the way so he could focus on the party. He told Squirt and Thadd to invite some people and that he wanted them to have a one-on-one with the last four girls. He got with the chef the next day and told him he needed food for about thirty people. He also made sure Angela ordered more liquor and champagne.

Wednesday night, Briell had dinner with all the girls. They dressed up and sat at an elegant table. They ate seafood and drank champagne. He told them about the party he had planned for tomorrow.

"What kind of attire should we wear?" Kendra asked.

"You can wear whatever you want. I just want all y'all to have fun and get turned, no cap." Briell answered.

"I'll drink to that." They put their champagne glasses in the air for a toast.

"To all of us for being at the villa with JaBriell." Jessica added.

"The final four." Joi smiled.

"Aye." They all cheer in unison.

CHAPTER 18

Thursday afternoon came quickly. The cases of alcohol arrived. The chef and his crew were preparing the food. JaBriell's barber had come to cut his hair. Angela even had Rachael and Candy come do the girls' hair and makeup. Angela also had balloons, lights and pool accessories sent to the villa. She paid extra for the delivery service to decorate both inside and outside. She told JaBriell she really wanted the party outside in the back area so not too many people would be in the villa for security purposes. She additionally hired more security guards.

Squirt and Thadd arrived early evening. Briell was happy to see his boys. Around seven p.m. the DJ set his equipment up on the patio. By eight p.m. the live feed for the show had started. About thirty people were present. The party was calm. People were dancing, but no one was in the pool. A few hours passed and Deek arrived This took the kick back from small and intimate to a full-blown party.

The pool was full of girls, while the guys kicked back in the jacuzzi. Deek streamed the party on his Instagram and his Facebook Live. People were still arriving. It was like a spring break party. The D.J. had everyone turned. It was at least one hundred people inside the villa and about two hundred people out back. Everyone was tuned into the show. Twitter was blowing up from viewers across the world. They had hashtag trending, #findingloveforjabriellpoolparty. The security guards stopped letting people in, it was so crowded.

Angela was freaking out. Dillard had left her side to be with some of his LGBT community. They ran out of food and alcohol, but Deek had someone bring twenty additional cases of liquor. The show was over, but the camera crew was still filming. It was after eleven p.m. JaBriell, Squirt, and Thadd were having the time of their life. Squirt grabbed the mic and the DJ cut the music.

"How's everyone feeling?" The crowd began to cheer. "I want to give a shout out to my dawg, my best friend Briell for throwing an awesome party and for him finding love. So, everyone take a shot for Briell." The crowds went crazy, and everyone downed their drink as the DJ starts playing music again. The party was going so well, Angela calmed down a bit. She even had a young guy dancing on her, and she was loving the attention.

The four remaining girls were also having a blast. They were dancing by each other, then JaBriell slid in between them, and they started dancing on him. There was a group of people playing volleyball in the pool. A few girls were on seated on guy's shoulders, a few of them even had their bikini tops off.

The party was still going strong at one a.m. JaBriell, Squirt, and Thadd were in the jacuzzi with five girls. They were smoking a hookah and drinking. Squirt soon left the jacuzzi with two girls and went into Briell's room. He locked the door so no one could disturb him. Thadd had a girl with him in one of the guest rooms.

By two a.m. the party was thinning out, but people were still there. The D.J. packed up at three, however the party goers turned on the so for sound system in the villa for entertainment. People were wasted, laying on the couches, and even the steps. There was was even a guy laid out under the pool table, there were people playing pool as if he wasn't there.

Dillard was still with his folks, hanging out in the pool. Angela was in her room with the door locked. It was almost four in the morning. One camera guy still filming. Everyone was almost all gone. The people that were there were either asleep or up talking. The camera man was looking for Briell. He went to all the girl's rooms. He wasn't with Jessica, Joi, Marissa or Kendra. The camera guy searched the whole villa for him. He finally was about to give up, until he went into the garage and found Briell asleep on a lazy boy chair by himself.

Hours later, Angela woke up out of her sleep. "Oh, my God." She said nervously. She jumped out of the bed and looked at her iPhone. There were no missed calls. "Thank you, Lord." She looked at the time. It read nine-thirty-seven a.m. She threw on some pants and a T-shirt. She put her feet in her slippers and walked out her room. The music was still playing softly. As she walked through the villa, it was a mess. There was a shirtless guy laying on the steps still asleep. Downstairs there was girls and guys asleep all over the couch. Angela turned off the music and then called Dilliard's phone. He didn't answer after several rings, so she hung up and called again. This time he answered after the third ring. "Dillard, where are you? And where's JaBriell?"

"I'm in my room, and I don't know where Briell is." Dilliard answered groggily.

"Get up and get downstairs now. There are people still asleep all around the house. We need to locate JaBriell and make sure the girls are good." Angela said with an attitude. Angela was looking at the big mess all around the villa. She grew madder every second.

"Damn, I'm going to get fired for this. I should have never agreed to him having a party." She scrolled through her phone list and called the cleaning company. When the receptionist answers, she informed them she needed a cleaning crew urgently. She gave them the address, and the receptionist told her the crew would be there within thirty minutes. Dillard soon came downstairs with a guy. They shared a hug, and then the guy left.

"I see you had a good night." Angela commented. Dillard didn't say anything. He started waking people up, instead. Angela ordered a, Uber to take anyone home that didn't have a ride. Angela's phone began ringing. Panic ensued when she saw it was Mr. Hopkins calling.

"Oh, shit. This is going to be a bad conversation." She thought out loud. She walked away from everyone and answered. "Good morning, Mr. Hopkins."

"It's a great morning. Have you seen the numbers for the show? It's better than last week's show, and he beat the record again. Damn, this boy is a star. Twitter is still going crazy about last night's party. There are all kinds of videos on IG and Facebook. Great job, Angela. Once he chooses who he wants to be with on the finale, we're going to do a spin off show. It will feature him and the person he picked. As soon as you guys are all wrapped up with everything next week, I want you and your team to come up with another show for him. There's never been a show like this ever. What you've done has never been done before. You have made history. Get next week over with, and I'll see you back in New York after that. Also, I'm sending Maria and her team down there on Monday. She's going to create two new commercials for the final episode. She needs to get with Henry for footage. Make it happen. Good work, Angela. We're proud of you."

"Thank you, sir." Angela said with relief.

"Whew." She exclaimed loudly as she walked back to where Dilliard was. He had woken everyone up that was downstairs. They were all leaving the villa. The Uber had just pulled up.

"The show broke another record last night. It's still the number one show in America." She explained excitedly.

"Oh my God, are you serious?" Dilliard smiled widely.

"I just got off the phone with Hopkins. He's ecstatic over the ratings and reviews. Where is JaBriell? And have you checked in on all the girls?" Angela rattled on.

"Yes, all of the girls are fine, and I went to JaBriell's room, but his friend Squirt was in there with two females."

Dillard and Angela look at each other and laugh. "Oh my. To be young again." Angela commented.

"Right. I even checked the guest room, and his other friend was in there with a girl." As they were talking, still wondering where JaBriell was, Squirt came downstairs with the two girls. He walked them out the door. Then Thadd and his guest came out the room and walked downstairs. When they got to the front door, they kissed, and the girl said, "Call me later."

"I will." Thadd said as she left the villa, he looked back at Angela and Dillard who were looking at him. "What a night." He smiled at them while yawning and stretching.

Squirt came back in the villa and looked at Thadd. They both smile at each other, and then they start laughing and dancing. Squirt sang the Kevin Gates song "2 Phones," but changed the lyrics. "I got two girls." He sang.

"Excuse me, Curly and Larry, where in the hell is Mo?"

Squirt and Thadd paused and noticed the seriousness on Angela's face.

"Who's Curly and Larry?" Squirt asked confused.

"Yeah, and who is Mo?" Thadd added.

"The Three Stooges." Dilliard said noticing Angela's frustration. He pointed to Squirt and Thadd and then said "Curly and Larry, and JaBriell is Mo. So where is he?"

"Oh, he's in the garage. He sent me a text last night and told me he wanted to get away from everyone and have some peace and quiet." Squirt informed them. Angela walked towards the garage and Dillard followed behind her. Squirt and Thadd followed along as well. When they entered the garage, JaBriell was still asleep in the recliner.

"I got to get this on a vine." Squirt said as he pulled out his phone to record.

"Yo, Briell." Squirt yelled in his face.

"Maria, I'm up." Briell said as he jumped out of his sleep. He looked closer, he saw it was Squirt recording him, and Angela, Dillard, and Thadd were standing behind him. He laughed and smiled.

"Stop recording me, you ass." They all laughed, "Angela, make him stop." Briell said asking for reinforcement.

"Squirt, give me that phone, boy." Angela said with a chuckle as she tried her best to be serious. Thadd helped JaBriell up from the chair and started play punching him.

"We had a great night. They're going to be talking about your party for years." Thadd said.

"Yo, I was in your room last night, you might want change the sheets." Squirt confided causing everyone to laugh.

"Go brush your teeth and meet me in the kitchen. Everywhere else in the house is a wreck. We have some good news to discuss." Angela said.

"Can I have my phone back?" Squirt pleaded.

"No." Angela said holding his phone up in the air.

"I'll give it back if you erase what you just recorded. I can't allow you to post that clip with him saying Maria's name." Angela explained further.

"We all know he loves her." Squirt retorted.

"Y'all know I can hear y'all, right?" Briell interjected. Briell then went upstairs and got himself together. The rest of them went into the kitchen. Angela and Squirt were still discussing the recording. Thadd opened the refrigerator and pulled out some eggs and bacon. He also pulled out some fruit. He went through the cabinets and found a flat pan with a handle and a skillet. He then grabbed some butter and found some seasonings as he began preparing breakfast.

Angela's text alert rang. She opened it up. It was an email from Hopkins. When she read the email, she screamed excitedly, "This is crazy."

"What now?"

"'The View,' Wendy Williams, 'The Talk,' and Steve Harvey all want interviews with JaBriell after the show is over."

"Get the fuck out of here." Squirt said shocked by the news. I'm serious. I'm reading the emails now that were sent to my boss. He just forwarded them to me."

Squirt says, "Angela, let me get my phone."

"That's not how you ask for something." She warned looking Squirt directly in the eye.

Squirt smiled and said, "Angela, may I please have my phone back? I'll delete that recording."

"That's better, and you better delete that recording." She said before giving the phone back to Squirt.

"Thank you. Now let me see what social media is saying about last night." He checked each of his social sites one by one.

"Damn, the hashtag #findingloveforjabriellpoolparty is still popping. Look at these tweets. Let me go to Deek's I.G." He scrolled to Deek's Instagram page to find that Deek had over twenty pictures and vines from the party. Every one of them had ten thousand likes or more.

"How is this possible? Briell is going to freak out when he sees this." Squirt exclaimed enthusiastically.

"Freak out about what?" Briell said as he entered the kitchen.

"Bro, you a freakin' star. Everyone is talking about you and the party last night." Squirt explained.

"He's right. Your show broke records again last night. It's the number one show in America. The party was a hit. Not only that, but *'The View,'* *Wendy Williams,* *'The Talk,'* and *Steve Harvey* want to interview after the show wraps."

"Steve Harvey, Steve freakin' Harvey." He screamed and hugs Angela.

"That's not all, JaBriell. After the show next week, me and my team have to head back to New York to work on another show for you. My boss called me this morning. They want to do a spin-off of this show. People want to know about you, your love life, and everything else. You're going to be a star."

"Is that another check?" Briell asked immediately.

"Yes, and honestly they have to pay you more than the first check. You're in demand." Thadd placed all their plates on the island.

"Let's pray before we eat." Angela offered. They bowed their heads as she prayed. After prayer they sat and ate together. Squirt grabbed two Moet Nectar bottles and popped them. He filled the flute glasses up. Before they could toast, the girls walk in the kitchen.

"Aye." They said in unison. They all smiled, and Briell hugged each of them, then Angela hugged them.

"Can we eat with y'all?" Jessica asked.

"Hell yeah, we have enough. And if we run out, I'll cook more." Thadd said politely.

"You cooked? Oh, Lord." Kendra said shocked causing everyone to laugh.

"Squirt, pour the girls some champagne. I have some good news for them." Angela said. Squirt grabbed the bottle and filled their flutes.

"Girls, the show has broken rating records, and it's the number one show in America right now. You'll are stars, just like Briell. Everyone is talking about you'll. They will be tuned into the finale. Believe me, each of you will capitalize off this show whether you win or lose. I suggest you all get agents which will help you get more opportunities, maybe even a sitcom or Netflix series. I will set something up for each of you next week. You will need help. I'm proud of all you'll. I'm not going to lie, that party last night was so crunked, I thought I was going to get fired."

"Turn't or lit, not crunk. That's old school." Squirt said educating Angela on the new school lingo. The group shared a laugh.

"I'm going to bust you up, Squirt." She said raising her fist up. They laughed again, before Angela resumed speaking, "Anyway, before I was interrupted, I'm proud of all of you. The camera crew will be here in an hour. I don't have any dates set up today, so today is a free day for you'll to do whatever. I suggest y'all do something fun together and enjoy the day."

Thadd made the girls' plates. They joined the rest of the group eating and drinking champagne. By the time they finished eating both the cleaning and the camera crews had arrived.

"Let's all go to the beach and kick it, rent some jet skis, paddle boats, and we can play a girls verses guys game of football."

"Yes, I got a fire bikini I haven't worn yet." Marissa exclaimed.

"Girl, me too." Joi agreed. The camera crew began filming. They got beach ready and headed out. Briell was in a good mood. He thought about Maria but didn't allow his thoughts to get his spirit down. He was blessed, and he knew it.

CHAPTER 19

The weekend ended and Monday morning came quickly. Maria and her team were on a plane headed to Tampa International Airport. Maria was nervous. She tried not to show her emotions. She developed a plan to not see Briell when she got there, at least until Thursday. She didn't know how that was going to work, but she was trying to avoid him. She didn't want to interfere with his decision up.

When they finally landed Maria and her team were walked through the terminal and headed to baggage claim to get their luggage. Once that was done, they got into the town cars and headed to Clearwater. They had room reservations for three suites at the Hilton. Maria placed Byron and Kenneth in a suite together, then Sharon and Cynthia in another suite, and her and Cindy shared the last suite. Cindy was Maria's right hand. She was to Maria what Maria was to Angela.

After they unpacked and got settled in, Maria ordered room service. When the food arrived, Cindy had steak and potatoes with broccoli. Maria had fried chicken, macaroni and cheese, green beans, and a waffle with syrup on the side.

"Someone is hungry." Cindy observed.

"I'm starving." Maria said taking a bite of her chicken leg. As they ate, Maria texted everyone and to let them know they would be heading out at two p.m. When Maria and Cindy were finished, they relaxed and watched television together. As one in the afternoon approached, Maria took a shower and began to prepare for the afternoon's events. She called Byron and reminded him to bring both the hard drive and his laptop. They would later view footage for the commercial, put the clips on the hard drive, and then transfer them to the Mac. Spotlight Productions was in Tampa off Adamo Drive. It took Maria and her crew forty-five minutes to get there. Maria immediately introduced her team to Henry.

"Glad to meet you all. Maria, how have you been, and where have you been? You've been missing all of the excitement." Henry said with a smile.

"I was promoted, I'm in charge of this side of the game, now. It's cool, I have my own team, and they make the marketing side happen."

"That's awesome, Maria. Let's go into the production room. I can't wait till you see the footage from the party. I know you'll be able to use a bunch of those clips." Henry said waving her in the direction of the production room.

"Let's get to it." Maria prayed she didn't see Briell messing around with a bunch of chicks. As they viewed the footage, Maria and Byron chose the clips they want to use. They watched the party footage with shock in their eyes. They couldn't believe the amount of people who were present.

"We definitely need some footage of the party." Maria exclaimed. They spent the next hour selecting footage from the party.

"This guy JaBriell doesn't let any of the women, the alcohol, or the partying get to his head. My camera guy Sam tried to catch him doing some dirt, maybe even with a girl. He waited until about four a.m. to try and catch him doing something, and this is what he found." Henry informed them as he began to roll the last clip. The clip showed JaBriell sleeping in the reclining chair by himself. Maria was so relieved; she was paranoid of what she may see. She was afraid the camera guy had caught him in the act, but when she saw him sleeping peacefully, she knew JaBriell was a good man, a man of integrity, the man she fell in love and wanted to be with.

"I'm actually convinced he's a good guy." Henry observed staring at the footage.

"Well, Henry, I think that will do." She looked at Byron and asked, "Do you have everything we agreed on?"

"Yes, ma'am." He returned.

"Ok, good. Henry, we will see you later this week. Have a good day, thank you."

"No problem. I'll walk you to the front." Henry said standing up and walking them out.

CHAPTER 20

Angela walked out of her room after a conference call with the producers and executives. She also called Maria to make sure her and the crew made it safely to Tampa. She made her way down the hall to JaBriell's room, where he was watching ESPN. She knocked on the open door to gain his attention. "Hey, Briell. Can I talk to you for a second?"

"Yeah, what's up? Did something change with this afternoon's date with Marissa?" He asked sitting up from his reclined position.

"No, no, everything is on schedule. I just got off the phone with the producers of the show and my executives. Since this is the last week, by Thursday they want to reduce the remaining girls to two. Today you will be eliminating one, and tomorrow you will send another one home."

"Damn, I wasn't prepared for that. That's going to crush the girls, but it's all a part of the show. I'll be ready to make my decision tonight." Briell said taking things in.

"Ok, great. I'll let you get back to your sports." Angela said as she backed out of the room. Briell sat in silence thinking. He knew he didn't want to get rid of Jessica or Joi, but he had a connection with Kendra as well. He knew tonight he would send Marissa home. He was glad they had another date today to kick it one last time.

The driver had arrived at the house and was waiting for JaBriell and Marissa. As they walked out the villa, the driver opened the door for them. They got into the truck and headed to Malibu. Once they arrived, they played miniature golf. Marissa was winning.

"Watch out." JaBriell screamed breaking Marissa's concentration. Marissa jumped and screamed while in motion of hitting the ball. He began laughing along with the camera crew. When she realized he was messing with her, she laughed and punched him in the arm.

"You scared me half to death." Marissa chuckled.

"Aww, poor baby." He said sweetly as he reached out to hug her. The two of them embraced and looked into each other's eyes.

"You did that on purpose, since I was beating your ass." Marissa teased.

"Yeah, I can't cap." JaBriell laughed a little.

"You gone play fair, or you gone continue to cheat?" Marissa asked kissing him on the lips.

"I guess I'll play fair." Briell said with a coy smile. She kissed him again and playfully pushed his head.

"You better." She said as they released their embrace. "Don't run from this whooping." She added as she got into position to hit the ball again. After their game of gold

"I had a really good time with you today. This was a great date." Marissa said as the two of them rode back to the villa.

"I had a good time with you, too." JaBriell said holding her close to him. Marissa laid under him the entire ride back. As they pulled into the driveway, he noticed another Escalade truck pulling out. He wondered who was in there. He woke Marissa who was sound asleep.

"I am so sorry. I was knocked out." She said with a stretch.

"It's cool. I dozed off too, it was good to have you up under me." Briell smiled.

"Thank you." She said graciously as they get out of the truck and go inside. Briell greeted the rest of the girls as they enter the house. They were on the couch drinking and gossiping.

"Marissa, did you have a good time with my man?" Jessica joked. Marissa shot her a look.

"The shade you throw." Joi commented shaking her head.

"Yeah, he was a real gentleman." She turned to Briell and kissed him on the cheek before saying "I'm going to make me a drink. Anyone else want one?"

"I do. What are you making?" Joi asked turning to her.

"A mimosa with strawberry in it." Marissa returned.

"That sounds good. I think I'll have one too." Kendra said standing up off the couch. The three of them walked into the kitchen together, leaving Briell and Jessica behind.

Jessica moved from the couch and stood in front of JaBriell. She wiped the spot on his face where Marissa kissed him and said, "I missed you."

"Did you really?" He asked with a slight smirk.

"I did, for real. I wish we were going on a date this evening instead of you and Kendra." She whined.

"I got you tomorrow." Briell said trying to cheer her up. She kissed him on the lips, and he returned her kiss.

"You better." She said as she walked away from him. "Let me get in this kitchen and see what these chicks talking about, I know they are hating."

"Be nice, please." Briell laughed.

"I'm always nice, baby. I'll be nice to you tonight if you let me in your room." Jessica winked.

"Maybe," Briell shrugged and smiles as she walks in the kitchen.

"Senorita Marissa, I know you're not tripping off what I said." Jessica said as soon as she reached the kitchen.

"Not at all. Your shade can't take away my shine. I had a good day and a good date."

"Mmm hmm. So, where did y'all go?"

"We went where we went." Marissa responded quickly. The girls laughed at her comment.

"I wonder where we're going." Kendra gushed excitedly.

"Can y'all believe Thursday is the last day? I done slick got used to living in this villa. Chef's cooking my food. The only thing I can do without is all the cameras following us and hearing everything we say." Joi added.

"You better get used to it. We're all popping right now. I'm definitely trying to be on another show." Kendra replied.

"Me too. I can't wait to get back in the studio and do my thing. This show has made my buzz and campaign go up." Marissa said with enthusiasm.

"It's definitely going to be exciting to see what our future holds. What about you, big booty Judy?" Kendra asked playfully as they all look at Jessica.

"I don't know what's in store for me and JaBriell. I just know we're going to be together, and if any of y'all hoochies win, I'm going to stalk y'all." Jessica teased. They all burst out laughing.

"Your ass is crazy, for real."

"Let me go take a shower so I can go on a date with my man." she said looking directly at Jessica, and t her the middle finger.

Kendra was a white girl, but she grew up around blacks her whole life, so she was up on point with the lingo. As she walked out the kitchen, she said, "Bye, hoochies. Talk to y'all later." They all said bye in unison.

Meanwhile, Briell was talking to Angela on the patio. "Have you told the girls yet about one of them will be going home?" He asked.

"No, I didn't want you and Kendra to have an awkward date. I'll let them know when you all get back. Sit down a minute, I want to talk to you about some things."

"What's up?" Briell asked taking a seat.

"How do you feel about doing another show? Will you be able to have someone look after your sandwich shop? You're going to be a very busy man. I just need to know if you're ready. I've renegotiated your contract with more money. I'm asking for one hundred-fifty thousand. High Rise can take you to the next level, but you must be ready.'

"I'm ready. I want the opportunity, I really do. But can I ask you a question?"

"Of course." Angela smiled slightly.

"Will I have these same opportunities without the girl I choose on Thursday?"

"Why would you want them without her? I'm just curious."

"Because I truly still love Maria, and when this is over, I want to see her, I need to see her. I need us to have a conversation. I need to know if I'm the only one feeling this way. Can you understand that? I mean, this is cool, but I'm basically flexing for T.V. Don't get me wrong, these women are beautiful, and Jessica is the only one I've kissed, grinded on, touched on, but I don't want to take it to the next level because of the way I feel about Maria. I feel as if I'm disrespecting her even though we haven't talked or seen each other. What we had was real, Angela, I know it was. I don't know if she had to back off from me because of this show, or maybe she just got scared because we both fell for each other so quickly. But I do know she still cares about me like I care about her, I can feel it." Briell explained.

They both sat in silence for a minute or so, before Angela said "Honestly, JaBriell, it's you that people love. The girl is just a plus. Can we just get through this week, pick who you like and go from there? Oh, and what do you mean by flexing for T.V.?"

"Putting on, make believe, making it look good for the camera." Briell laughed; he'd forgotten Angela wasn't up to date with the latest lingo.

"Oh, well, you're definitely a good actor. Keep flexing for the camera, the ratings are through the roof. We will figure everything out next week after this show is done, I promise." Angela assured him.

"Ok." He said before standing up to walk away.

"Don't give up on Maria or your love for her." Angela called out behind him. JaBriell nodded his head in agreement.

"Oh, and I forgot to tell you, you and Kendra will be going bowling and skating, so can you let her know so she will dress for the occasions?" Angela added.

"I got you." Briell said as he headed towards Kendra's room. When he arrived at the door, he pushed it open.

"Kendra." He called out as he walked in. Kendra was in the mirror doing her hair in some sexy printed boy shorts and matching bra. "My bad. I'm so sorry, I should have waited for you to answer before I walked in."

"Don't be silly. Come in, close the door." Kendra invited. JaBriell did as he was told and closed the door. He couldn't help but stare at Kendra's sexy body. She had a big butt for a white girl, and it was looking great in those boy shorts. She noticed him looking at her. She puts the brush down and faced him.

"Do you like what you see?"

"Hell yeah. I didn't know it was like that." Briell smiled.

"Well, since you're in here, can you put some lotion on my back?" she asked grabbing the lotion and walking towards him, licking her lips.

"Not only is Kendra beautiful, but she's sexy as hell too." JaBriell thought to himself taking a deep breath. *"Control yourself. You can do this."*

Kendra handed him the lotion, and he squirted some in his hand and starts to apply it to her back. Her body was smooth. She still smelled fresh from the shower. As he rubbed the lotion in on her lower back, he put more lotion on his hands and rubbed the back of her legs and slowly moved up to the bottom of her butt cheeks that were sticking out from the boy shorts.

"That feels good. You know how to use those hands." Kendra complimented. His face was so close to her butt he wanted to bite it, but he controlled himself.

"All done." He said as he stood up from the bed.

"Thank you. "Kendra said as she began applying lotion to her arms.

"Did you want to tell me something?"

"Oh yeah, I got thrown off track. Um, Angela said we're going to the bowling alley and then skating."

"Really? I haven't been skating in a long time. This is going to be great."

"Cool. I'm going to get ready, and I'll see you in a minute." He looked at her one last time and said, "Damn, girl. You just don't know."

"Bye, JaBriell."

An hour later, they left the villa and headed to the bowling alley. Their date went well. They both won games at the bowling alley, and they loved the skating rink. Kendra and Briell laughed and joked like two teenagers in love as they held hands skating together. JaBriell fell once and Kendra laughed, and when she went to help him up, she fell on top of him. They had a blast.

After they skated, they ate pizza and chicken wings and drank a pitcher of beer. Briell was shocked at how cool Kendra was on this date. His connection with her had gotten stronger, maybe just as strong as his connection with Jessica.

The date ended and they headed back to the villa. Once they arrived, without any delay Angela sat the girls down and told them to get dressed for the ceremony tonight because JaBriell had to choose one of them to go home tonight. They were all in shock by the news.

"I guess one of y'all are about to pack up." Jessica before walking away to get ready. The other girls looked worried.

"Don't worry, we all had a great run." They each got up and went to their rooms to get ready. As they all got dressed, they couldn't shake the nervousness. Some of the girls even paced back and forth in their rooms. They were not prepared for this, but it was time to face the music.

The girls assembled in the room the show began in. JaBriell complimented them as he entered the room. "Over this past month I've grown to care about all of you. I've connected with all of you on different levels. This is hard for me, to send one of you home. Jessica you will be staying with me in the house."

"I told y'all." Jessica smirked. She walked to the other side but not before touching Briell's chest.

"The second person who will remain in the house is Joi." Joi smiled and took a deep breath. She moved to the other side with Jessica, stopping to touch Briell's arm in the process.

"This is a hard decision because I've have truly connected with both of you, but I only can choose one of you to stay with me at the villa." He took a deep breath and looked at the last two beautiful women in front of him. "The third person that will be staying in the villa with me is Kendra." Kendra placed her hands over her face as tears stream down.

"I'm sorry, girl." Kendra said with a hug before moving to the other side with Jessica and Joi.

"Marissa, I had a great time with you. We had a little chemistry, but the connection wasn't as strong as the other girls. You're beautiful, and I wish you all the best of luck." JaBriell spoke sincerely.

"Thank you." She said in a solemn tone.

"Finish up that EP, and I'm going to be the first person to buy it, I promise." JaBriell said hugging her.

"Thank you so much for that." Marissa said with tears in her eyes. The remaining girls all gathered around and hugged her. They had formed a tight bond throughout their time in the house.

CHAPTER 21

Tuesday morning, Briell woke up in a weird mood. He wasn't happy that he had to send Marissa home. He was also thinking about Maria. He was beginning to think maybe he should let it go and date Jessica. She was the one he liked the most. Then Angela's voice rang in his head, reminding him not to give up on Maria or love.

With that reminder he jumped out of bed to take a shower. After the shower, he got dressed and went downstairs. It was early, so no one was up yet. He decided to shoot some pool alone. He racked up the balls and hit the white ball into the formation. He was ten minutes into his game and Kendra came downstairs. She grabbed a pool stick and joined him.

"Thank you for saving me last night. I know that was hard on you." Kendra said warmly.

"It was. I even woke up in a funk. I had to shake it off. That's why I'm up so early. I'm trying to clear my head."

"Do you want to be alone?"

"Nah, I need the company." He said hitting the cue ball again, and the red ball misses the corner pocket. "I just don't like to hurt people's feelings. I know everyone won't win, but it still bothers me. Your shot." He revealed.

"This has been a great experience for me, whether I win or lose. I met an amazing man, and I know you and I will remain cool."

"Thanks, Kendra, and I think you're amazing too, and yes, we will be cool."

"I'm going to hold you to that." She said taking her shot. They finished their game and went into the kitchen. Kendra cooked JaBriell some breakfast, and when they sat down to eat.

"Good morning." Jessica said entering the kitchen. Briell and Kendra, both greeted her. Jessica walked up to Briell and kissed him on the cheek and grabbed one of his pieces of toast and took a bite.

"Who cooked?" Jessica inquired.

"Kendra did. It's good, too." Briell said.

"Thanks for cooking for my man, Kendra." Jessica smiled.

"No problem. I had to feed him after our morning game. Oh, he beat it well with that long stick. See y'all later. He's all yours, Jess." Kendra said before grabbing her plate and exiting the kitchen.

Jessica was heated. Briell smiled and shook his head left and right. "Y'all are crazy." Briell said with a slight chuckle.

"Nah, she's about to catch a beat down." Jessica bellowed.

Briell grabbed her around the waist and said, "Don't get yourself all worked up. We have a date today."

"Ok, baby." She said softening up.

"That's better." Briell said patting her on the butt. He kissed her causing her to blush. "What's that look for?" Briell asked looking into Jessica's eyes.

"Because that's the first time you ever kissed me, first."

"Maybe I'm starting to like you a little bit." Briell said with a smile.

"A little bit?" Jessica said punching him in the chest.

"Oh, Lord. What am I going to do with you?"

"Oh, I have some things you can do to me." Jessica said causing them to both laugh. "Where are we going today, Daddy?"

"I don't know yet. I have to ask Angela. I don't know if you're my first date today, or the last date. I can't wait to spend some time with you, either way." Briell and Jessica started making out in the kitchen but were soon interrupted by Angela walking in.

"Do y'all have to do that in the kitchen?" Angela frowned. The two of them stopped kissing for a minute and greeted Angela.

"Well, I'll let you two talk." Jessica said as she turned back towards Briell and kissed him.

"Let me know about the date." She smiled grabbing a handful of his manhood. "And let me know about him too."

"That girl has the hots for you. You act like you really like her." Angela observed. She then looked at the camera men and said "Y'all give us a minute, please. Go and film the girls."

"Yes, ma'am," The agreed leaving the kitchen.

"Today will be the same as yesterday. After your dates you will have to send one of the girls home. I know it's hard and not fair, but it's business. How are you feeling?" Angela said quickly.

"Like a jerk. But like you said, it's business. I'll be ok. What's up with the dates today? Am I going with Jessica or Joi first." Briell asked cutting to the chase.

"You and Joi will go first, and then you and Jessica. You and Joi will go to Busch Gardens, and you and Jessica will go to Adventure Island. Both of those places are in Tampa, so all three of you will leave together, there are two rooms on reservation at the Hilton. Jessica will stay in her room and wait until you and Joi are finished. After. Your date with Joi ends you will return, refresh, and get ready for the next date. Here's a question for you, If Maria were here, do you think you could play the game as well as you're playing it with these girls?" Angela asked.

"No, I couldn't" JaBriell confided.

"Do you understand why Maria couldn't be here? Think business, JaBriell. This is almost over. You have two more days. Anyway, when is the last time you've been to Busch Gardens and Adventure Island?" Angela asked switching the subject.

"It's been a couple years since I've been to Busch Gardens, but we went to Adventure Island last year. Growing up, we liked Adventure Island better."

"I don't think I could do that water that much, but I would love to go to Busch Gardens." Angela returned.

"Maybe you can visit before you return to New York."

"Nah, we have no time for that. We have to get this money." Angela said high-fiving JaBriell.

"Let's get, get, get it." JaBriell cheered as he left the kitchen. He stopped by Joi and Jessica's rooms and told them the game plan. Angela waited until the coast was clear to pick up the phone and call Maria.

Hey, girl. How did the edits for the commercial turn out?" she asked as soon as Maria greeted her.

"It went good. I'll send them to your email. Both of them are done and in rotation on the networks."

"Great job, I see you, girl. What time will you be here on Thursday?"

"I don't know, maybe towards the end of the show. I don't want things to be awkward with me there.

"Maria, I'm going to keep it real with you. That boy is not happy without you. It is what is. He's only doing the show for business purposes. He knows he wouldn't be able to play the games as well if you were here. Hopkins was right about not sending you. He needs to see you, though. I think he's starting to like Jessica. That will change once he lays his eyes on you. I told him just to pick a girl and we'll go from there." Angela rattled on. Maria was quiet. Her mind was on Briell and wondering about this Jessica girl.

"Maria, you still there?" Angela called out to her.

"Yeah, I'm still here. I was looking at something."

"Oh, girl, handle your business. We'll see each other soon."

"Ok, talk to you later." Maria said as the call ended.

Within the hour, Briell, Jessica, and Joi were headed to Tampa. Briell and Joi had a blast at Busch Gardens. Briell and Jessica had an even better time at Adventure Island. Hours later, the dates ended, and they headed back to the villa. Soon as they returned, Angela broke the news to the girls once again that one of them would be going home tonight. Kendra was freaking, she believed since JaBriell spent the day with Jessica and Joi, they would have a closer connection to him.

"Oh, my God," Kendra screamed placing her hands on top of her head. She was frustrated to the max. Jessica just walked to her room and got ready. She was confident that Briell would pick her.

It was time for the girls to walk into the ceremony room. Briell was already waiting for them. Once they entered, Briell spoke, "You all look so beautiful. This is the part of the show I hate the most, but I have to send one of you home tonight." He took a deep breath and spoke again, "The first person I choose to stay at the villa with me is Kendra." Kendra walked over and stood on the other side of the room.

"The next person that will remain in the villa with me is Jessica." Jessica hugged Joi, then Kendra came over and hugged her, too.

"You're a wonderful person. It was great spending time with you." Briell said as he hugged her tightly.

"Thank you." Joi said as they hug again, and she leaves the ceremony room.

The chef brought Briell, Jessica, and Kendra champagne glasses, and Briell said, "Let's make a toast." They all raise their glasses, and he smiled, "To the final two."

"To the final two." They Jessica and Kendra said as they drank the contents of their glasses.

CHAPTER 22

Wednesday morning came fast. Angela gave Briell and the girls the day to relax. Around 10:30 a.m. the doorbell rang. Angela heard it but didn't move. She figured someone downstairs would get it. Briell heard it as well. He figured the same thing, that someone else would answer it. One of the camera guys answered the door, and Thadd and Squirt stood on the doorstep along with four girls. The guy remembered Thadd and Squirt from the party.

"What up, bro?" Squirt said as he walked into the villa without being invited. Everyone else followed behind him. The girls had grocery bags in their hands, and Thadd had two duffel bags in his.

"Yo, yo, yo, is anybody home? Where's my dawg Briell at? Where's Angela at?" Squirt yelled. At the sound of his voice Angela opened her eyes. She knew that voice.

"Oh my God, what is he doing here?" Angela said aloud. Briell opened his eyes and smiled. He knew his homeboy's voice. Thadd and Squirt ran upstairs to his room. They bust in his room, rushed to his bed and start play punching him and urging him to get up. Their loudness woke everyone up.

Briell got up and started wrestling with them, and as Angela was walking in the room, he had Squirt in the headlock and Thadd was about to jump on the two of them.

"What are y'all doing here?" Angela asked. The guys froze and looked at her as if she was their mom. The three of them looked like scared kids, which only made Angela laugh.

"It's too early for this." Angela said shaking her head. They each got up and looked at each other.

"Angela, we've come to aggravate you." Thadd said as he began to act like a zombie. Briell followed suit acting like a zombie also.

"Get her." Squirt called out in a zombie like voice.

"Y'all better not start." Angela said as they neared her. "I'm serious." She reiterated as the got even closer. Still, they maintained their zombie act walking towards her. Briell got closer and acted as if he was about to bite her. She screamed and laughed while running out of the room. The camera guys were filming everything. The girls were in the hallway laughing.

"Get them all." Briell ordered the zombie crew. Jessica and Kendra ran into Angela's room with her. The boys walked into Angela's room, still acting like zombies. Squirt started play attacking Angela, while Thadd attacked Kendra and Briell attacked Jessica. They were all screaming and laughing while the boys were on them, except Jessica. She loved the fact that Briell was trying to bite her.

"Bite me baby, yes." Jessica screamed playfully. The camera guys were laughing hysterically. After a few minutes, they stopped. They were all breathing hard and winded.

"I knew I could make you laugh, Angela. Be happy." Squirt smiled. Angela couldn't deny it. She had had fun with the guys. They were sweet.

"Get out of my room." She ordered instead of agreeing with Squirt.

"Such a killjoy" Squirt grimaced.

"Now." She said pointing to the door. As they all walk out of Angela's room, Briell looked at Angela and growled. She growled back, and he smiled.

"What am I gone do with these kids?" she said aloud.

"Briell, this is Teka and Isabell." Thadd introduced as they arrived downstairs.

The two girls smiled, and spoke in unison, "Hey."

"And this is Toya and Tonya. I call them TNT because they're the bomb." Squirt introduced excitedly. They laugh, as they greet Briell.

"This is Jessica and Kendra." Briell introduced his final two ladies to the group.

"We know who they are. We love what y'all are doing on the show." Teka added.

"Yeah, Jessica, you're doing your thang, girl, you be having us dying laughing." Toya said sweetly.

"Yeah, girl, you don't play." Tonya chimed in.

"Where's the other two girls, Marissa and Joi? It was four of y'all last week." Isabell asked confused.

"What you see is what you get, and they didn't get picked." Jessica informed them.

"We're the queens of the house now." Kendra said proudly. The guests were shocked, even Thadd and Squirt.

"Damn, Briell, what happened to them?" Thadd asked with a look of shock.

"You got to watch the show Thursday and see." Briell shrugged.

"Come on, bro. We yo dawgs." Squirt groveled.

"Anyway, what's good? What's up with the grocery bags?" Briell said looking around.

"Oh yeah. Today is freaky beach day at Clearwater Beach, it starts at two p.m. We figured y'all would want to join us, and we bought some chicken, hot dogs, sausages, and hamburger meat so we could cook on the grill before we head out."

"Hell yeah, let's do it. I'll have one of the chefs fire up the grill." Briell said anxiously.

"I love freaky beach day." The boys said as they dapped one another.

"Briell, is there a room we can put our bags in, and where we can change before we head out?" Tonya asked.

"Yeah, there are plenty of rooms. Jess, can you show the girls which room they can use, please?"

"Yeah, baby. Y'all follow me." Jessica agreed. All the girls followed Jessica, while the guys and Kendra go into the kitchen.

"Damn, I forgot none of the chefs are here until later."

"It's cool. You know I'll get on the grill." Thadd replied.

"Alright then, bet. Kendra, can you help season the chicken and ground beef?"

"Yeah, I help my dad all of the time when we grill." Kendra agreed.

"Kendra can cook for real." Briell complimented.

"Alright bet. Let's get it going then." Squirt added. While they prepared the food, Squirt played some music through the Beat speaker.

"Can I help do anything?" Isabell offered as the other girls returned to the kitchen.

"Yeah, can you make us some mimosas? We love those things." Briell told her.

"What's a mimosa?" she asked confused.

"Let me show you." Briell said walking over the wine refrigerator. He pulled out two bottles of Moet along with orange juice and strawberries. He gets a knife and says, "Go wash these strawberries right quick." Briell said handing her the carton of strawberries. Briell showed her the quick easy steps to making a mimosa. Isabella followed each step creating Mimosa's for the group.

"Damn, this is good." Everyone agreed as she handed out glasses.

Kendra and Thadd just finished cleaning and seasoning the chicken. They were now about to season and make hamburgers.

"Thadd, get me two eggs, and see if there's some minced garlic in the refrigerator." Thadd did as she asked, he opened the refrigerator and grabbed two eggs a jar of minced garlic. When he handed them to her, she got a big bowl and began to mix all the ingredients together. Together they made big hamburgers, chicken, brat sausages, and hot dogs.

~ 154 ~

"This is a lot of food to cook." Thadd observed looking at all the food on the countertop. He walked out onto patio and fired up the grill. Once it was hot enough, he put the chicken on. The girls were on their third glass of mimosas. They decided to get in the pool while the food was cooking. Angela joined them on the patio, she laid on a lawn chair and began tanning. She wore a two-piece bikini. She had a scarf tied on her head, with a pair of sunglasses, she looked beautiful. Squirt walked over to her and handed her a mimosa.

"Thank you." She smiled. Squirt stood in front of her shirtless. He had on a pair of swim trunks and Jordan flip flops. His trunks sagged a little, showing off his Tommy Hilfiger boxers. He stared at her body with lustful thoughts. He knew Angela was pretty, but he never knew how thick and sexy she was. She tilted her sunglasses up and looked at Squirt.

"What, Squirt? Is there something I can help you with?"

"Nah, I'm just enjoying the view. I didn't know it was like that."

"Well, now you do." Angela sneered pulling her sunglasses back down.

"Hmph, with your sexy mean ass." Squirt said still standing in front of her.

"Your young ass wouldn't know what to do. Go entertain your guests." Angela said with an eyeroll.

"Oh, I know what to do with it. You need some young meat in your life. Then you wouldn't be so mean." Angela couldn't believe the way Squirt was flirting with her.

"I'm not mean. Keep talking crazy, I'll show you what your mouth can do."

"On that note, I'm leaving." Squirt laughed.

"Yeah, get your young ass out the way. You're blocking my sun."

"You can get that too." Squirt said licking his lips and looking between her legs.

"Bye, Squirt." She smiles as he walks away and shakes her head left and right.

By mid-afternoon the food was ready, and the group had begun eating. Thadd had done a great job. The food was a hit amongst the crew. did a good job, and the food was good. Kendra had also done a great job with seasoning and preparing everything. There was plenty of food to go around, even the camera crew ate well. Once everyone ate, the girls went to take showers and prepare for Freaky Beach Clearwater. Briell was trying his hardest to convince Angela to come with them.

"What is Freaky Beach Clearwater? It sounds like it's bad, like Freaknik or Black College Spring Break in Daytona." Angela said frowning her face.

"I don't know what Freaknik or Black College Spring Break is." Briell said confused.

"Both are before your time, Dear."

"Well, Freaky Beach is an event where vendors come from all over, there are games, food and music, it's like a carnival of sorts. There is something there for everyone. You should come along. We only have one more day here, at least have some fun before you

"Ok, fine. I'll go." Angela said with a deep breath.

"Good, now get up and get ready. We're heading out in about an hour." An hour and a half later, everyone was dressed and ready to go. Briell was dressed in a white and orange printed Polo T-shirt with tan cargo shorts, on his feet he wore a pair of orange and white Lebron sneakers.

Squirt had on a Vans T-shirt with acid wash light blue jean shorts and navy blue and a pair of white Vans on his feet. Both the girls and the guys looked good for the occasion. Each of them came ready for the occasion.

"Damn, Angela, you look good." Jessica complimented admiring Angela's Gucci ensemble. The other girls agreed with Jessica each giving Angela a compliment as well. Angela felt good for her age, she still had it going on.

"Where is Henry?" Angela questioned looking around.

"He's loading the van. He's ready when you guys are."

"I want two of you guys on Briell, Jessica, and Kendra the whole time. The other two cameramen can film us."

"Yes, ma'am." The camera guy agreed.

"Are we ready?" Angela asked.

"Yeah," The group said in unison, and they all head outside.

"As good as you look, I may have to take you up on that mouth offer." Squirt said to Angela with a wink.

"You don't know what to do down there." She shot back.

"You can teach me." Angela looked at him and smiled and before getting into the Escalade. She was flattered by Squirt's flirting. She was also interested in his tongue action. His last comment turned her on.

On the way to the beach event, Angela called Dillard who was back in New York working with coworkers on JaBriell's next show. He left a couple days after the party at the villa.

"What's up, girl?" Dilliard answered cheerfully.

"Oh, nothing, just hanging out. Listen, I need you to email me six non-disclosure agreements. Add a clause that details the recipients will not be compensated for their appearance. I'll text you all the names now."

"I'm on it. Soon as you send the names, I'll get it done."

"Thanks, Dear. How's everything else going?"

"It's going good. Everyone is excited to see what the numbers are for the last week. Hopkins is thinking about doing the next show in Tampa; however, he would like to send Briell and the person he chooses on a vacation somewhere tropical. "Dillard explained.

"Sounds expensive, but exotic. Well, let me get those names, and I'll talk to you later." Once they disconnected Angela began to explain to Thadd and Squirt and that their guests that they would have to sign a non-disclosure agreement. She gathered their legal names and all the information that she needed as they rode to the beach. Just as they arrived at Clearwater beach, she texted all the information to Dillard. Henry and the camera crew began to prepare for filming.

The cameras drew so much attention as beach goers pointed and stared. It didn't take long for fans to begin asking for autographs. Girls were asked if they could take pictures with JaBriel, while both male and female fans asked to take pictures with Jessica and Kendra.

As the day went on, they played games. Briell won Jessica and Kendra a stuffed animal. They came upon a dunk-a-friend booth, if you could dunk your friend, you could win a big stuffed animal. No one in the group wanted to be dunked.

"I'll do it." Squirt said bravely as his friends begin cheering him on. He took his shirt and shoes off and got into the booth. He sat on the board, and Angela says to the guy

"How much is it?" Angela asked the attendant.

"Five dollars for three tries." He informed her. She handed him five bucks and stood on the line to throw the ball.

"You can't dunk me, Angela." Squirt teased. She tried not to pay him any attention as she threw the first ball, she missed by an inch. All the girls cheered her on, along with Briell and Thadd. People passing by stopped and watched. The guy gives her another ball.

That was just a warmup. You're going down now." Angela winked as she grabbed hold of the next ball.

"Don't talk about it, just do it."

Angela moved back to the line, she looked at her target and threw the ball hard and fast. This time she didn't miss, Squirt fell in the water. Everyone standing around cheered for Angela as she laughed at Squirt. The attendant handed her a huge stuffed mermaid. Squirt climbed out of the dunk booth; he was soaking wet. The attendant gave him a towel and he proceeded to dry off.

"Ha ha." Angela chuckled in his face.

"Whatever. You did that, I can't cap." Squirt grinned.

"I played softball in college." She admitted before walking away. They stayed at the beach for another hour. As they were leaving, they stopped at the funnel cake stand, and Angela ordered everyone one. Angela handed Squirt his funnel cake last.

"You still mad at me?" She smiled.

"I wasn't mad at you, it was fun. You still a meanie, but I'm glad you had a good time."

"How old are you, Squirt?" Angela asked as they walked back to the Truck.

"I'm 25. Why?" Squirt answered back.

"Just wondering." She shrugged. They returned to the Escalade, and everyone was said how hungry they were. Angela called the chef and told him to prepare a meal for twenty people. On the way back to the villa, they made a stop at a local printer so Angela could get copies of the non-Disclosure agreements. They arrived back at the villa an hour later.

"The chef cooked for us. If you all want to freshen up, take a shower and then eat, or eat first and then freshen up, it's cool with me either way. I'm going to take a shower first." Angela informed the group.

"Me too." A few of the girls agreed. The guys followed suit.

After everyone finished freshening up, they met in the dining room and sat at the table. They were eagerly awaiting the chef serving them dinner. They were all drinking Ciroc, with either pineapple or cranberry juice. The vibes around the villa were great. They were each sharing their experiences at Freaky Beach amongst the group.

Angela caught Squirt looking at her several times. One time she silently mouthed, "What," and he stuck his tongue out. She smiled and laughed at his gesture.

"This boy is so persistent. Should I let him taste me?" She thought to herself. She tried her best to push the thought out of her mind, but the more she drank, the more she thought about his face between her legs.

"I'm going to get another bottle." Briell announced as they finished the first bottle.

"Is it me, or is Angela really pretty as fuck?" Squirt asked Briell as he followed him into the kitchen.

"Nah, it's not you. Angela is a baddie. She's shutting a lot of young girls down."

"For real, right?" Squirt agreed.

"Why?" Briell asked.

"Nothing. I'm just amazed at how beautiful she is." Squirt explained.

Briell grabbed the bottle of Ciroc while Squirt grabbed some more pineapple juice before they return to the dining room."

"She's out of your league, Buddy." Briell said patting Squirt on the back.

Briell refilled everyone's drink as he returned to the table. The chef entered with hot plates for everyone. Everyone's eyes widened when they saw the lobster ravioli pasta. It smelled delicious.

"Everyone let's join hands, I'm going to say a quick prayer." Kendra said. Everyone joined hands and bowed their heads as Kendra said a prayer. When she was done, they said Amen as a group, picked up their forks and dug in. The chef brought out salad and fresh baked bread sticks. They ate like kings and queens, and when they finished eating Briell asked everyone to kick it around the bonfire.

Thadd had gotten the hookah out of his car for them to smoke. He had different flavors. The girls roasted marshmallows while they listened to music and relaxed.

"Briell, I will see y'all later. Teka, Isabell, Tonya, and Toya, it was a pleasure meeting you. Thadd and Squirt, I am sure I will see you two before I leave. Jessica and Kendra, we have a big day tomorrow. Try not to party all night. Y'all be good, I'm tipsy." Angela said as she stood up to exit. The group wished her a good night and laughed at her comments at the same time.

"Thanks for allowing us to be on the show." Tonya said.

"No problem, girl. It's all good." She smiled at Tonya. "Squirt, I'm about to lay on that mermaid I won from dunking your ass." She laughed along with everyone else. Squirt even laughed. She leaves and goes up to her room. She takes her yoga pants off and laid on the bed in her T-shirt and panties.

The rest of the group continued to take shots. An hour later, everyone went back inside. Briell put out the bonfire.

"I don't want y'all driving back to Tampa, y'all can just stay here. If any of the girls have to leave, I can have the driver take y'all back to Tampa."

"I'm good. I'll stay." Isabella said.

"I'm good, too." Teka said.

"I want stay, but me and Toya have to be at work at eight a.m." Tonya said.

"And we can't be late. Our boss already be talking shit about us." Toya added.

"It's cool. It won't be a problem for the driver to take y'all home."

"It was a pleasure meeting y'all." Kendra said as she hugged both Toya and Tonya.

"It was good meeting you, too." They agreed.

"We did it big today. I'm glad y'all came. I had so much fun." Jessica smiled as she hugged the two of them.

"Thanks, girl. We had fun too." Toya said.

"No cap, today was off the hook, and we're going to be on the show, aye, aye, aye"

"I'll get y'all bag and walk y'all out." Squirt said. Teka and Isabell hug Toya and Tonya. Briell hugged them as well. Squirt then walked them outside to the car with Briell. Briell instructed the driver to take them back to Tampa.

Y'all text me when y'all get home." Squirt said as they prepared to pull off. The girls agreed.

"I'm out. I'm going to bed. Thadd, you can take the guest room, and Squirt, you can sleep on the couch or in Marissa's old room." Briell offered.

"I'll take the room." Squirt said heading in the direction of the room. Squirt couldn't sleep. He had Angela on his mind. He finally got the nerve to go to her door. The house was quiet. Everyone was asleep. He could hear the television on in Briell's room, and music playing in the room Thadd, Isabell and Teka were in. He tapped on Angela's door; she didn't answer right away so he tapped again.

"Who is it?"

"Squirt." He whispered.

"Why are you still here?" She asked as she stretched and yawned. Squirt caught a glimpse at sexy Victoria's Secret panties as she lifted her arms. Squirt explained how Briell didn't want them to drive home after drinking so much. As he was talking, she turned around and got back into the bed. He nervously closed the door and walks in her room.

"Man up and give her what she wants." He said to himself as he took off his shirt and climbed in the bed from the bottom. He slid under the comforter and slowly kissed on Angela's leg. His tongue slowly moved up to her knee. He opened her legs and then sucked on her inner thigh passionately. He switched to the other leg and kissed close to her love box. He moved her panties to the side. He couldn't believe how good she smelled. He put his tongue on her clit and licked it. It started to feel good to Angela. She opened her legs wide as he put his face all the way in her box. He sucked on her clit like candy. She softly moaned.

"Take my panties off." She instructed him in a low seductive tone. He removed her panties and stared at Angela's beautiful body. She grabbed his head and put it back between her legs. He began sucking and blowing on her, again.

"Ooh, that feels good. Do it like that." Angela cooed. She began to rock her hips in the same motion as his tongue.

"Suck on it." She ordered and he did what he was instructed. Angela was moaning and screaming. He began flickering his tongue on her, driving her wild.

"Yes, don't stop." Squirt continued to satisfy her until she climaxed.

"Let me give you some more. I'm trying to put it in your ass." He spoke.

"Oh my God." Angela moaned as Squirt began giving her head until she climaxed all over again. He turned her over and moved her towards the end of the bed and lifted her butt in the air. He slipped on a condom before putting his manhood inside her. He pounded her faster and faster. The deeper he went the more she loved it. Angela was moaning loudly as she put her face in the pillow to stifle her voice. The liquor only intensified his drive. He flipped her over on her back and put her legs behind her head and entered her again. Angela became even wetter; she hadn't had this feeling in years.

"Oh shit, oh shit." She screamed as Squirt continued to thrust into her. He could feel his own climax coming, but he didn't slow down. He continues to go in and out of her. The more he stroked the wetter she became. When he could no longer hold it, he busted inside the condom and slowed down his stroke. He slowly went deep inside her. She moaned and threw it back.

"Damn." He moaned, through sweating and heavy breathing.

"That was good. That was the best." He said aloud still in a daze. They both laid in silence for a moment. Angela couldn't believe he made her cum so many times. She felt Squirt's hands opening her legs again, soon his face was back down between her thighs. Before she could say anything, he was giving her head again. He was going for round two, and she didn't put up a fight.

CHAPTER 23

Thursday morning Angela awoke to find Squirt still in the bed with her. She quickly woke him up and said, "You have to get out of here. I don't want everybody in my business."

"Alright." Squirt said as he rolled out of bed groggily. Angela got out of the bed and went into the bathroom. She washed her face and brushed her teeth. She turned on the shower jets and let them run.

"Damn, Angela, you're even beautiful in the morning." Squirt said as he walked up behind her in the bathroom.

Angela was slightly bent over on the bathroom counter looking in the mirror. She only wore her panties and bra. Squirt couldn't resist the urge to hug her from behind.

"Thanks for last night. Now be nice today." He whispered in his ear. She could feel his manhood poking her through his boxer briefs.

"You're welcome, and I'll try."

Squirt started kissing on her back, while grabbing another condom and slowly putting it on.

"Squirt, what happened last night, was last night. I'm not going to be having sex with you like this."

"Let me get that good stuff one more time." He soothed her kissing her on the back of her shoulder blade. "Please." He begged.

"Ok, hurry up." Angela said giving in. He bent her over and entered her from the back.

Thadd was in bed with Isabell on the right side of him and Teka on the left. He looked up at the ceiling and smiled. He had a vision of last night's episode. He had two beautiful women by him, and he didn't want that moment to end.

Kendra had got up and decided to cook breakfast for everyone. She washed her face and brushed her teeth, and then put some clothes on and went downstairs to the kitchen. She began pulling out the pots, pans, and skillets. Angela walked into the kitchen and noticed Kendra getting breakfast started.

"Good morning. Do you need some help?" Angela asked.

"Um, yeah, that would be great." Kendra responded surprised by Angela's offer.

"Let me make some coffee and I'm all yours."

"Ok." Kendra said spinning around to face Angela. She was in a surprisingly good mood this morning. Kendra continued to prep everything she needed. Angela started the coffee maker and noticed the Beats speaker box on the counter. She connected her phone and turned-on Ella Mai's album. The song "Good Bad" started playing. As she made her coffee, she sang along to the lyrics while dancing. Kendra looked at her and laughed, before joining in singing the song as well.

While they made breakfast, Jessica came downstairs and heard them. She walked in the kitchen and saw Kendra and Angela cooking breakfast. When Angela saw Jessica, she cheerfully said, "Good morning."

"Good morning. You're awfully happy." Jessica observed.

"I am. It's the last day." Angela returned; the truth was she wasn't happy it was the last day. She was happy because she had the best sex, she'd had in years last night. Squirt made her cum five times last night, and the quickie he gave her this morning started her day off better than any cup of coffee.

Kendra and Angela had the villa smelling good, the aroma of fried fish, shrimp and grits, biscuits, eggs, French toast, regular toast, and cut up pieces of fruit filled the air.

"Jessica, can you wake everyone up, please, and tell them breakfast is ready." Angela requested.

"Ok," Jessica said quickly as she headed out of the kitchen to wake everyone else up. Kendra went to set the table and place the food on it. Within ten minutes, everyone was downstairs at the table. Briell was at the head of the table with Jessica on his right and Kendra on the left.

Briell said grace, and they started eating and talking. Angela explained the details of their last dates. He and Jessica would go ATV riding on a dirt road course, and he and Kendra would go zip-lining and practice mountain climbing. His date with Kendra was first.

After she finished telling them about the day's events, Isabell began talking about how much she had fun when she went zip-lining. While everyone was either eating or listening to Isabell's story, Squirt put his hand on Angela's leg. She acted normal, and he began to feel her box. Angela played it cool, everyone at the table was oblivious to what was going on. After everyone finished eating, they all helped clean the table and the dishes. Briell and Kendra soon began preparing for their date.

"Hey Angela, I understand if you have to send Teka and Isabell home, but I want Thadd and Squirt to stay. I want my friends here with me for this last show." Briell explained as he and Kendra neared the door.

"I have no problem with that, Briell, and if Thadd's friends want to stay, they can. My focus is you, Jessica, and Kendra. They'll be fine here. Go on your date and make your last connections." Angela smiled warmly.

"Thank you, Angela. Thank you for everything." Briell said with a hug.

"You're welcome." Angela returned. Once Briell and Kendra left, Angela went to inform Thadd and Squirt that Briell wanted them to stay for the ceremony. She also informed them that Isabell and Teka could stay as well. The boys gave each other some excitedly.

"Do you twowant to stay until after the ceremony this evening?" Thadd offered.

"Hell yeah." They said in unison.

"I need some clothes. I can't be looking like yesterday." Isabell added.

"Facts. We need to hit the mall up right quick." Teka agreed.

"That's cool. I need to something too." Thadd informed Squirt that he and the ladies would be going to the mall. He invited him to join them. Squirt ran upstairs to holla at Angela before they stepped out.

When he reached her room, he knocked on the door and awaited her answer.

"Come in." she called out from behind the door.

"Hey, me, Thadd, Teka and Isabell are about to go to the mall. Do you need me to bring you something back, or do you want to go?"

"I need some accessories for tonight. Maybe I should go." She said looking up in the air.

"Well, if you're going to go, everyone's getting dressed now, go ahead and get ready." Squirt urged her.

"Ok, cool."

"We were going to take Thadd's car, but if all of us are going we'll probably need to take the other Escalade."

"That's no problem."

"Aight, bet. I'm about to go get ready."

"Thanks for inviting me and making sure I was good." Angela said as he prepapred to leave the room.

"No problem. Thanks for being nice." Squirt winked.

"Whatever." Angela smiled. Within the hour they were in the mall shopping. Angela was surprised that Thadd had enough money to buy him, Isabell, and Teka clothes and shoes. She was even more surprised that Squirt paid for her accessories.

Once the girls finished shopping, it was time for Thadd and Squirt to get their things. Angela went to the ATM and got out two hundred dollars. When she got back with the group, she secretly handed Squirt the money. She felt like since he paid for her things, she would surprise him and pay for his clothes. The guys went to shop together, and the ladies went to Victoria's Secret to get some panties and bras.

"Can I ask you all a question?" Angela asked as they browsed the selections together.

"Yeah, what's up?" Teka and Isabell answered.

"Are you both are seeing Thadd?"

"I know it seems weird, but we both like him, and we're not going to go behind each other's back and sleep with him" Teka said maturely.

"How did y'all meet?" Angela dug deeper. Both the girls laughed at her question.

"We were joking around with him while he was drunk at a party, actually the same night Squirt let everyone know Briell was single." Isabell disclosed.

"Oh, that party." Angela nodded her head.

"So, how does it work? Can he talk to anyone he wants, can you two have other men, and how long do you think this will last?" Angela said firing off back-to-back questions.

"Honestly, we're just having fun. I don't know all the rules to this game. This has been going on since before we were born, friends have been sleeping with the same man for years. Hell, men do it all the time. If he or any one of us ever finds that right person to be with, I'm sure we will part ways. I'm at a point in my life where I just want to have fun, hang out and kick it. I don't want the whole Netflix and chill thing. I just want to kick it with my girl, it just so happened that we found Thadd, and he just wants to have fun too." Isabell summed up.

"Thadd isn't a man whore. He has a good job, he respects us, he's not thirsty, he's that type of guy me and Isabell love to be around, so why not smash him together?" Teka reasoned.

"I guess if it works for y'all, then it is what it is. One thing I admire about you two is what Isabell said, you have enough respect for each other not to go behind one another's back and sleep with him. A lot of women do that, especially to their friends. So, I get it, just have fun. Lord knows I need that." Angela revealed sweetly.

"You should let Squirt be your boy toy. I've noticed how he looks at you. Hell, maybe you can change his life, make him get a job, be responsible. Don't get me wrong, he's hella cool, but he needs some guidance. He needs a woman like you, not to be your man but to get you right when that box needs attention." Teka finished.

"It's amazing the power we have." Isabella added

"How old are y'all?" Angela asked.

"I'm twenty-three." Teka answered

"I'm twenty-three also, but I'll be twenty-four next month."

"We've known Thadd, Briell and Squirt our whole lives. The five of us grew up in Town and Country. Out of all the guys to be with, they're the ones. They're the good guys." Teka explained further.

"How old are you, Angela, about twenty-eight, thirty?" Isabella guessed.

"Thanks for the compliment, but I'm forty." Angela giggled.

"Wow." Both girl's jaws dropped.

"No way." Teka marveled.

"Are you serious?" Isabell said enamored by how good Angela looked.

"Yep." Angela assured her.

"Girl, you look damn good for your age. I would have never imagined you were forty." Teka admired.

"Black don't crack. I'm glad I have some of it in me." Isabell went on. The three of them shared a laugh.

"Do y'all like these?" Isabell asked holding up a pair of panties.

"They're cute." Teka squealed.

"They are cute." Angela agreed. After shopping around Teka and Isabell put their items together to check out. Once they checked out, Angela paid for her items right behind them. She was amazed at how inexpensive Florida was compared to New York.

When they walked out of the store the guys were standing there waiting for them. Teka and Isabell began talking to Thadd about what they bought.

"Let me carry those bags for you?' Squirt offered extending his hands.

"Thank you." Angela smiled.

"No, thank you. Don't be trying to spoil me." Squirt teased her.

"Oh, I know how to get my money's worth back." She laughed sticking out her tongue.

"You're not going to use me for my mouth services."

"Watch and see." Angela returned before picking up the phone to call Henry. She wanted to check on Briell and Kendra. He informed her that everything was going well, and they would be heading back to the villa shortly.

"Ok, if I'm not back at the house when you all arrive, tell Briell Jessica to get ready for their date and head out soon as possible. I want them all to have ample time to relax before the ceremony.

"Will do." Henry agreed before disconnecting the call.

"Angela, I just have one more store to go to and then we can leave."

"It's cool. Take your time. We can eat when you're done. I want some mall food. I haven't had it in a while." Angela responded.

"Angela, let me find out you're balling on the low, talking about you haven't eaten mall food in a while." Teka remarked nudging Angela.

"I do alright, girl." Angela said with her hands on her hips. They shared a laugh as Thadd headed to his last store.

Briell and Kendra were headed to the Escalade. They were laughing and talking about the zip-lining. Henry relayed to them what Angela said, and they head straight back to the villa.

By the time Angela, Thadd, Squirt, Isabell and Teka get back to the villa, Briell had already left with Jessica.

"Hey, Kendra, how long have Briell and Jessica been gone?" Angela inquired.

"Over an hour." Kendra informed her.

"Ok, good. How are you feeling? Did the date go well?" Angela asked. Kendra was blown away by Angela's questions. She had never been this nice.

"I'm feeling good, and our date was amazing. Thanks for asking." Kendra replied politely.

"No problem. I'm going to relax." Angela said as she exited the room.

"Thadd, can we show you what we bought from Victoria's Secret?" Teka enticed.

"Hell yeah." Thadd smiled.

"We want to put on a show for you." Isabell seduced even further.

"I'm ready. Let's go." Thadd said rubbing his hands together. Meanwhile, Squirt was downstairs in the kitchen making a drink when Angela walked in and grabbed a bottle of Bellaire Rose

"Open this for me. I'm going to relax in the jacuzzi. You can join me if you want." She invited as she grabbed the Beats speaker and headed to the patio. She puts on some R&B music and got into the jacuzzi.

A few minutes later, Squirt walked out on the patio with two champagne flutes and the bottle of Belaire in an ice bucket. He sat the flutes down and pops the bottle. Slowly, he poured a glass of champagne for Angela and handed it to her. He then got inside the jacuzzi and settled on the opposite side.

"This feels so good."

"Yes, it does and it's peaceful." Angela agreed with him. Squirt reached out and grabbed her foot, he began massaging it.

"Thank you. "Angela smiled.

"I like you better this way." Squirt said still massaging her foot.

"What do you mean by that?

"You're more relaxed, and nice. I knew that was what you needed." Squirt said.

"I did. I can't lie, you put it down. But best believe it takes more than sex to make a woman relax and be nicer. Sometimes my job can be very demanding. It can make a person mean and uneasy. I've had a great time on this assignment. I have to let you know, I'm not this little girl that you can dickmatize and hen treat any kind of way. I appreciate the sex and everything else, but I'm a grown woman, and I need more. And I'm not saying this to make you think I want that from you. I'm just saying in general, and I feel you're grown enough to understand where I'm coming from." Angela explained.

"I understand, and believe me, I know you're having fun with me. I'm having fun with you. I can honestly see myself with you, giving you what you need beyond sex. I know you're older, and I think I need a woman as mature as you to mold me into the man I need to be. Some days I feel like I need to leave Tampa, to become a better man."

"How do you know it's me you want to be with. Why do you feel you can give me more. I mean, we already had sex, what more do you want?" Angela asked.

"Sometimes you just know. Sometimes you just get that feeling. When I see you, I want to talk with you and when we talk, I want more conversation. When you leave, I want come to New York and see you." Squirt confessed.

"What exactly are you saying, Squirt?" Angela asked looking in his eyes.

"I'm saying that I want to date you, I want to visit you, I want to possibly be your man." Squirt said sincerely.

Angela took a sip of her champagne and looked at him in his eyes. He looked back into her eyes; his eyes were soft, and he radiated sincerity.

"Is that what you really want, Carlos? Are you ready to be that man? Are you ready to give up all this young ass around here and be with me?" Angela asked testing him.

"Truthfully, I'm not smashing everything moving. I tried to be with the in crowd, have multiple women, but I didn't like it. When I met you, it was different, and your sex is incredible. It's the best sex I ever had, hands down. You're killing those young girls." Squirt complimented.

"You're so pretty, your smile is beautiful. I know we have an age difference, but I don't care, and I don't care what anyone else would think either." Squirt went on.

His hands slowly went up her thighs, and his fingers were exploring in her box as he finished his last words. Angela's legs slowly opened, inviting his fingers into her wetness. He was about to move closer to her when Thadd jumped down in the jacuzzi, followed by Teka and Isabell.

"What's up, y'all? What y'all drinking on?" Thadd said.

"That Belaire, boy." Squirt shot back.

"Rose." Thadd sang.

"Angela, do you mind if we have some?" Isabell asked.

"Of course not, there's another bottle in the fridge. Go and get it along with some champagne flutes." Angela said pleasantly. Isabell did as she was told going into the kitchen to retrieve the bottle and champagne flutes.

"It's been a pleasure, guys, but I have to get ready for tonight. Briell will be back within the next hour. Oh, Teka and Isabell, Candy and Racheal are my makeup and hair stylists. They will be here soon. When they're done with me, Jessica, and Kendra, I'll have them make sure that you two are good as we ll.

"Thank you." They answered in unison. Angela got out of the jacuzzi and pulled the bikini bottom out from her butt.

"Damn, Angela, I didn't know you had all that back there." Isabell commented. Angela blushed and grabbed her towel.

"Y'all are too much. Y'all two keep me laughing though." She grabbed her bottle and headed back inside the villa.

A few more minutes passes and Briell and Jessica returned. Kendra came downstairs to get Angela's phone for her. She greeted Briell and Jessica on her way to the patio.

"Where are my boys at?" Briell asked.

"They're in the jacuzzi. I have to run upstairs and take Angela her phone. She was stressing about how she left it out there." Kendra said rushing past the two of them.

The doorbell rang alerting Briell. It was Candy and Rachel; they had arrived to prep the girls and Angela for the ceremony.

"Girl, I have the perfect hairstyle for you tonight. You're going slay." Candy said as they hugged Jessica.

"Ok, ok, you know this is going to be my man after tonight, so you have to make sure I'm dripping, sauced up, for real." Jessica squealed with excitement.

"Oh, I got you." Candy responded.

"Where's Angela? I've been calling her." Rachel said looking around.

"Oh, her phone was out on the patio. Kendra just took it to her." Jessica explained.

"Let her know we are here. We're going to set up in our usual spot." Rachel told her.

"Okay." Jessica said as she kissed Briell and headed upstairs to let Angela know Candy and Racheal were there.

"What up, my brodies?" Briell greeted as he walked out onto the patio.

"Aye. "Squirt and Thadd returned in unison. Briell smiled and walked towards the jacuzzi. He spoke to Teka and Isabell and then said to Squirt and Thadd, "Man, y'all get out the jacuzzi and come help me pick out what to wear tonight."

"Alright, bet. We're on our way." Squirt said. Briell picked up the Rose bottle and drank straight off the top.

"Turn up, turn up, turn up." Thadd cheered.

"Aye, aye, aye." The girls chimed in the background.

"I'm about to pipe up." Briell said with a little dance.

"Pipe up then, Bro." Squirt encouraged.

"Y'all come help me. We're going to pipe up later." Briell smiled.

, "Alright, bro, we'll be right there." Briell went back inside the villa and upstairs. Thadd, Squirt, Teka and Isabell dry off before they walk inside the villa. As Squirt and Thadd passed through on the way upstairs the doorbell rang, again. Squirt walked over and opened the door. His mouth fell wide open, and he froze as if he'd seen a ghost.

When Thadd saw who it was, he backed down the few stairs he's walked up.

"Maria." Squirt said still confused by her presence.

CHAPTER 24

"**H**ey, Squirt." She greeted.

"What's up? Where've you been?" He asked as the rest of her team entered the house and began to set up.

"The bosses put me in charge of another department, so I had to do what I had to do." She shrugged.

"I feel you." Squirt nodded his head.

"Hola senorita Maria." He walked up to Maria and hugged her.

"What's up, Thadd?" she greeted in return.

"We've missed you, and someone else missed you, too." Thadd disclosed.

"Who you do you have here with you?" Squirt said changing the subject.

"Oh, where are my manners? Squirt and Thadd, this is Byron, Kenneth, Sharon, Cynthia, and Cindy. Guys, this is Squirt and Thadd. These are JaBriell's best friends." Maria introduced. They spoke to one another and shared a round of handshakes.

"Where is Angela? I've been calling her." Maria said stepping further into the house.

"Her phone was out on the patio. She had it plugged into the Beats speaker." Thadd explained.

"She has it now." Squirt said.

"She's upstairs. Come on, I'll take you up." Thadd invited.

"You guys can have a seat. Make yourself at home. I'll be right back."

Squirt hurried up the stairs to make sure Briell was in his room, and not in the hallway. As Thadd and Maria walk up the stairs, Squirt burst into Briell's room. He had clothes laid out on the bed.

"Which one do you think I should wear?" he asked.

"Uh, let's wait until Thadd comes in before we choose."

"Ok. Why you acting so weird?"

"Nun, dawg, I'm good. We're good." Squirt said peeking his head out of the door. He watched as Maria went into Angela's room.

"She's in Angela's room." Thadd blurted as he walked into the room.

"Who's in Angela's room?" Briell asked confused.

"Let's just pick out your attire for tonight." Squirt said trying to change the subject.

"Look, man. We need to tell you something." Thadd confessed.

"Tell me what?" Briell said with his eyebrow raised.

"About these outfits. I don't know which one you should choose." Squirt confessed.

"Squirt, he needs to know what time it is." Thadd reasoned.

"Yeah, it is getting late. We better get you dressed." Squirt said still committed to keeping Briell out the loop.

"Maria is here." Thadd alerted Briell.

"Lord, please bless us." Squirt shook his head.

"My Maria?" Briell asked trying to confirm what Thadd had just said.

"Where is she?" Briell asked walking towards his bedroom door.

"Take a deep breath. Remain calm and don't overreact about this." Thadd said trying to calm Briell down.

"Please Dawg, just chill. Come sit down." Squirt plead.

"Did y'all know about this?" Briell asked looking at Squirt and Thadd with anger in his eyes.

"No." They both said quickly.

"Come on, bro. We would have been told you if we knew. You have to believe us." Squirt assured him.

"We know how much you love that girl. We just found out, for real. Right before we walked upstairs, the doorbell rang, Squirt opened it, and she was right there." Thadd explained.

"That's what happened, no cap." Squirt confimed.

"I need to see her, Man. I can't choose one of these girls. What am I supposed to do?" Briell said taking a seat on the couch.

"Go on with the show. You said it yourself; the plan was for you to pick one of these girls and then be with Maria. You signed a contract. You have to do the last ceremony. I'm pretty sure y'all will be able to talk after the show. Just be patient, and don't freak out."

"Angela." Maria called out as she entered her bedroom. Angela was in the bathroom; she didn't hear Maria come in.

"Oh shit." She said in a low tone.

"Maria, is that you?" Angela said stepping into the doorway.

"Yeah, I've been calling you. I'm here early." She explained to her. Angela moved into her bedroom and hugged Maria.

"Sorry I missed your call. My phone was on the patio." Angela told her.

"Yeah, Thadd told me. I hope I arrived before Briell got in from his last date?"

"Umm, not exactly. He's two doors down." Angela said.

"Oh my God, oh my God, oh my God. What if he doesn't want to see me? What if he really likes one of these girls? I have to tell him why I left. I have to tell him I love him." Maria panicked.

"Calm down, baby. Don't work yourself up. Just breathe. Here, sit down on the bed. Now look, after the show, you and Briell will have all the time you need to talk. Just be patient." Angela soothed. Angela's text alert went off. She walked over to the dresser to check it. There was a message from Squirt asking her to meet him in the hallway.

"Maria, sit there, don't move. I'll be right back." Angela instructed as she walked out the room. Squirt was standing in front of Briell's door.

"Why didn't you warn us Maria was coming? Briell's freaking out. He wants to see her." Squirt murmured to her as soon as she was in ear's reach.

"She was supposed to come later tonight, and she's freaking out too. She thought he would still be on his date. She wants to talk to him. I don't know what to do. I told her Briell had to do the show and they could talk afterwards."

"I told him the same thing." Squirt informed her. Angela's robe wasn't fully closed. Squirt looks at her sexy body adorned in a pretty bra and panty set.

"Damn, you look good." He complimented her.

"You weren't supposed to see those until later. Wait, what am I saying? Focus, Carlos. You have to keep Briell occupied until the show. I'll keep Maria with me." Angela said taking a deep breath.

"Ok, but what about her team? They're downstairs."

"Ok, tell Thadd to keep them company. Get them some drinks and have him show them around the villa. They can't know this is going on. Can you handle that?" Angela asked.

"I got you, baby." Squirt said sweetly. They looked at each other, and then kissed.

"We can't be kissing right now. Our friends need us." Angela said with her hands on Squirts chest to create space between them.

"You're right, but damn, those lips." He said before trying to go in for another kiss.

"Carlos." Angela warned.

"Ok." He conceded before going back in the room with Briell. Angela went back down the hall to her room with Maria.

"Where is she? Can I talk to her?" Briell asked anxiously as Squirt entered the room.

"Bro, you got to trust me. You have to stay calm." Squirt looked at Thadd and said, "I need you to go downstairs and entertain Maria's team. Get them all some drinks. Show them around the villa while we sort this out. We don't need them to get suspicious of the situation. Angela will be down there shortly."

"Ok, I got you." Thadd nodded his head with confidence. He left the room immediately and headed downstairs.

"Sorry for the wait. Angela and Maria are discussing some business. She asked me to get you guys something to drink and show you around the villa. Follow me to the kitchen, let's pour up some drinks, shall we?"

"Alright," one of the agreed.

"I need a drink." Cindy chimed in. "I thought maybe Maria got sick again. She's been feeling under the weather."

"Oh no, she's fine." Thadd assured her. When they reached the kitchen Thadd poured them all a drink.

Angela's phone began to ring. She looked at the caller ID, and saw it was Candy calling. *"Damn, I forgot to call her back."* She thought to herself as she answered.

"Hey, Candy. I'm sorry I didn't have a chance to call you back." She spoke immediately.

"That's cool. We're all set up. Can you send Jessica or Kendra downstairs so we can start on one of them or both if they're out the shower and getting dressed?" Candy requested.

"Okay. They'll be down in a minute." Angela retorted.

"Maria, don't move. Promise me you won't move. Don't worry about your team, either. Thadd is making them some drinks, and then he's going to show them around the villa. Just sit here, I'll be right back." Angela instructed as she prepared to leave the room.

"Ok." Maria nodded her head. She was staring in space, with one leg shaking as she bit on her fingernail.

"Candy and Racheal are ready to do your hair and makeup. Have you showered?" Angela asked Kendra as she barged into her room.

"Yes, I have. I'm ready." Kendra said.

"Ok. They're downstairs in the same spot they did your makeup and hair before." She announced as Kendra prepared to leave the room. Angela walked down the hall to Jessica's room and told her the same thing. Jessica had just gotten out the shower.

"Can you tell them that I'll be down in 10 minutes?" Jessica requested.

"Ok, but hurry." Angela urged. Angela walked back to her room where Maria was still frozen in place. "I'm going to get dressed, and then we will go downstairs together. Is that okay?" Angela asked looking at Maria.

"Okay." Maria nodded, again.

Angela dressed in a tight-fitted Versace dress showing off all her curves. She puts on her accessories and comes out the bathroom and sat next to Maria.

As she's putting on her black Jimmy Choo shoes, Maria spoke, "I have a bad feeling I've lost him. I can't handle seeing him all boo'ed up with some other girl. I shouldn't have come over today."

"Don't think like that, Maria. I know firsthand that JaBriell loves you. He loves you more than any of these girls." Angela stood to check herself in the mirror and then walked over to the door. She peeped her head out to make sure the coast was clear.

"Come with me. Let's get our face and get our hair done." She looks Maria in the eye and says, "You look like you've been stressed. Pull it together, Baby. You are strong, you are fierce. Get your shit together, I mean it." Angela said lifting Maria's head.

You're right. I don't want him to see me like this. I want him to want me, just like he wanted me before I left." Maria smiled and spoke.

"That's my girl. That's the confidence I was looking for. You got this." Angela cheered her on. They walked out of the room and downstairs to let Candy and Racheal start on their hair and makeup. When they entered the room Candy and Racheal were just finishing up Kendra's look.

"I love it." Kendra said looking at herself in the mirror.

"You look great, Kendra." Angela admired.

"Thank you. I'm going to go and finish getting ready." Kendra said before exiting the room

"Come on, Diva. You're next." Candy said inviting Angela to her chair.

"Angela, you're slaying that dress, you look like you're about to walk the red carpet." Racheal complimented.

That's how I'm going to be feeling when Briell picks me. Me and my man are going to be waving bye to the haters like we're on the red carpet." Jessica announced.

Maria's face morphed to anger when Jessica said that. She was furious, and Angela quickly saw it. She hurriedly changed the subject. "Racheal, do you remember Maria, can you do her hair and makeup, also?"

"Yeah, I remember that beautiful face. I'm almost done with Jessica. I got you girl." She assured.

"Thank you."

Racheal was finally done with Jessica, she went back upstairs to finish getting ready for the evening. Maria sat in the chair, and Racheal began to work her magic on her.

Squirt and Briell had finally decided on what he should wear. He chose the J. Lindeberg suit. The suit was black with blue pin stripes. He rocked a white button-up shirt underneath the jacket with a black tie. Tucked in his top pocket was a white handkerchief and his wrist were adorned with shiny silver cufflinks with blue gems in them, along with a diamond watch with a matching blue face. His shoes were made by Delavan and pulled the look together.

As the ladies got their hair and makeup done, Briell was getting dressed. Kendra and Jessica were putting the final touches on their look. Thadd was still entertaining Maria's team. Teka and Isabell were dressed and were waiting for Angela and Maria to get finished in the chair. Everything was going smooth. Maria had calmed down, and Briell got himself together.

When Angela was finished in the chair Teka took a seat. Henry walked in to speak with Angela. They walked out the room, and he informed her that they would be going live in forty-five minutes.

"Are you ready for me to get everybody in position?" Angela asked.

"Yes, as soon as possible. Once we go live, we will go directly to the ceremony. We will have the girls talk about their experience in the house and being with JaBriell. The last thirty minutes will be all about him making his final decision.

Angela went upstairs to get Kendra and Jessica, but first she knocked on Briell's door. Squirt opened the door wide allowing her to view Briell. "Wow, boy, you look good. That suit is fly, good pick." Angela complimented with a smile.

"Squirt actually picked it out." Briell said nudging him.

"Ok, Squirt, I see you."

"I see you too. Versace, Versace." He smiled admiring her outfit.

"We need you downstairs within the next ten minutes." Angela said reeling the guys in.

Maria's hair and makeup were finally done, she stood from the chair. Isabell was about to sit down next. Maria stared at her briefly before speaking. "You're beautiful. You should have been on the show."

"Thank you," she smiled politely.

"That's one of the bosses of the show. She makes shit happen." Rachel said looking over at Maria.

"Thanks again for the compliment, and thanks Racheal, thanks Candy."

Maria excused herself from the room and headed into the kitchen. She was hungry. She asked the chef to make her a grilled turkey sandwich. Henry was in the ceremony room preparing the lights for the show. Kendra and Jessica were on their way downstairs. Henry had two seats for them to sit down and talk about their experiences on the show and journey with Briell. Candy entered the room to do final touches before they went live.

Thadd and Maria's team had finally made their way back to the villa. They went into the kitchen to get a refill of their drinks.

"Maria, this place is amazing. I wish we could have stayed here for a couple of days." Cindy said as she watched Maria enjoy her sandwich.

"It is beautiful." Maria responded coyly.

"Twitter is going nuts about Briell sending Joi and Marissa home. The viewers are tuned in. The ratings should be good tonight." Cindy added.

"It would be awesome if it breaks last week's numbers." Sharon chimed in.

Angela walked into the kitchen and was greeted by hugs. Everyone complimented her on how great she looked.

"Twitter is going crazy already." Byron informed her with his glass in his hand.

Briell walked downstairs with Squirt. He took his position in the ceremony room and awaited the beginning of the show.

"We go live in five minutes." Henry said as he walked into the kitchen.

"Now, I have the baddest women in the house. Y'all look good." Thad complimented as he laid eyes on Teka and Isabell. Teka and Isabell smiled at his compliment.

"Thank you." They said in unison.

"Take your time and come out when you're ready." Angela said to Maria in a low tone.

"Okay, I will." Maria replied.

"5, 4, 3, 2,1." Henry counted down before pointing to the interviewer. Kendra began speaking as Briell scanned the room for Maria. He spotted Angela, but Maria was nowhere in sight. He was wondering why Maria didn't want to see him. He didn't understand what he did to her. He wasn't feeling good about their relationship. He had doubts about everything. He tried to focus as Kendra finished and Jessica began speaking. Minutes into Jessica's interview, he looked in the crowd again for Maria. He still didn't see her. On the outside he was trying to keep it together, but on the inside, he was hurting, his heart was aching.

The interview came to an end, and the interview spoke boldly into the camera, "Well, ladies and gentlemen, we have now arrived at the moment we've all been waiting for. JaBriell, will you please stand?" JaBriell stood to his feet just as Maria exited the kitchen. She stood next to Angela.

"Kendra and Jessica, will you please stand and take your positions?" the interviewer continued.

Jessica and Kendra both stood. JaBriell's head was down, as he lifted it he scanned the room once more. His heart stopped as he laid eyes on her standing next to Angela. She looked more beautiful than ever. She looked as if she were glowing.

Maria instantly had tears in her eyes. The man she fell in love with and missed so much was standing right before her. He looked good in his suit. It was like he was the only person in the room."

JaBriell, would you like to share anything about the woman you're about the choose?" The interviewer asked.

"The first time I laid eyes on her, I said wow, this is the most beautiful woman I've ever seen in my life. When we got to know each other, she made me smile, she made me laugh. The feeling I got from this woman was real. Not only is she beautiful, but she's smart, independent, and kind. She is the person I desire to spend the rest of my life with. The times we shared were amazing. I fell in love with her." JaBriell said as his eyes began to water, and tears streamed down his face. JaBriell's speech only made women all over the world fall deeper in love with him. Twitter was going crazy with comments.

"I'm still in love with her, and I need her to know that I'm not afraid anymore. I want to be more than friends. I want to be her best friends. I want to be her husband, I want us to have children, and I want everyone in this room and all the viewers to know that I choose," JaBriell paused for a minute before walking in Angela and Maria's direction.

"I choose Maria Vasquez. This is the person I truly love." He declared. The whole room stood still. No one could believe what just took place.

"I love you and I miss you so much. I'm sorry if I ruined the show. I had to let you know how I truly feel."

"It's ok, I love you too. I never wanted to leave you. Everyone felt it would be best if I weren't here. I have never stopped loving you, though." Maria spoke through tears. The two of them kissed as everyone applauded. Jessica stomped away angrily. The love JaBriell and Maria's shared brought tears to the eyes of almost everyone in the room.

"JaBriell, Maria, come and sit down. America wants to know your story." The interviewer called out.

"What's going on?" she asked as they took a seat before her.

JaBriell and Maria both smiled as they were holding hands. JaBriell spoke up first. "I met Maria about two and a half months ago. She accompanied Angela to Tampa to pitch the show to me.

"So, you all met right before you met all the girls for the show?"

"Yes, she actually helped to choose the girls." Briell explained.

"At that time, we were still on a professional level. I can't lie, I was checking him out. He's such a handsome guy.

"When did sparks begin to fly between you two?" The interviewer asked.

"For me, the sparks were already there, but they really started to fly one night while I was out with my friends, Thadd and Squirt," Briell paused because Squirt was objecting from across the room.

"Yo, yo what up, bro?" Thadd and Squirt called out in unison.

"As you can tell, that's them over there." Briell chuckled.

"The three of us went out to celebrate me signing on for to the show. I sent her a video of us wilding out at the strip club. She sent a text back that made me laugh, and of course I texted back, and before you know it I was told her that we were going to IHOP. She then asked if I could bring her some food." Briell finished.

"That 3-in-the-morning food." The interviewer chimed in as if she could taste the food. Everyone in the room started laughing.

"I brought her some food, and she was a true lady. She didn't invite me inside her hotel room. We met in the hallway in front of her door and talked a little bit, and then I left. That's when the sparks started flying for me." Briell smile widened.

"What about you, Maria?"

"That's how I started to like him as well. He was so sweet and such a gentleman."

"Let's get to the juicy stuff. When did the romance start?" The interviewer pried.

"I began to like her even more when I realized my little sister also liked her, and she doesn't like anyone. I loved the way Maria interacted with her. We would talk every day, not just through text, but talk. When I did the 'Good Day America' I was nervous, and she helped me through it. Afterwards, we arrived at the villa to shoot the first commercial, and for some reason we always were left alone with each other."

"It's crazy. It was like it was meant to be, especially when we were alone in the villa."

"Oh, so you all had this whole place to yourselves?" She said looking around.

Yes." The two of them sang.

"That's when it came unprofessional." Maria admitted.

"I bet." The interviewer confirmed causing everyone to laugh again.

"Is this really true love? Can you fall in love in three months?" she wondered aloud.

"I didn't believe Briell had fallen in love with me at first, but his actions have shown me he did. The connection we had was like never before."

"I have to agree. The day she was going back to New York I was sick. I missed her so much, especially when she told me she wasn't coming back. My world was turned upside down when she told me we could no longer see each other. I thought she played me." Briell sighed.

"I had to. The pressures of a job can make you crazy and unhappy. I had to choose my job or him. I also had just gotten a promotion, so I chose the job. I was miserable, though. I missed my best friend. I missed his conversation. I missed his lips." Maria wooed. Maria and Briell looked at each other and kissed. The audience went crazy.

"This man is worth it." Maria enthused.

"And she's worth it too." Briell said as he placed his arm around her shoulder.

"I have to tell you something. I need to know that you were serious about being my husband and having kids." Maria said looking into his eyes.

"Absolutely." Briell said with confidence.

"I'm pregnant." Maria said shocking everyone.

"That's why she's been sick in the morning and hasn't been drinking." Cindy whispered to Sharon.

"Are you serious?" Briell asked filled with emotion.

"Very serious. I'm six and a half weeks today." Maria explained.

Angela passed the interviewer her phone and she observed the screen, "Well, JaBriell and Maria, America loves you. The show is trending on Twitter. They want you and Maria to be together. I can't lie, this has been the best show in a long time, and Briell, you put the ultimate twist on it. No one in a million years would have thought you'd pick the girl that works for the company that hired you. Neither did Jessica. Let's show America how she looked when you chose Maria." The interviewer said pointing to the monitor. Footage of Jessica crying and storming off, prompted everyone to laugh.

"I am rooting for you guys. I pray everything works out for you both, and I speak for all the viewers, when I say we want to see more of you guys. I hope there's another show."

"Thank you." Maria and Briell spoke in unison.

"Well, America, we are out of time, and we are pleased to announce that JaBriell Gibson found love. Please comment and use the hashtag. Thanks again for watching the show. Good night."

"5, 4, 3, 2, 1, and we're off." Henry yelled.

Angela ran over to Maria and Briell and hugged them both. "It was worth it. I know Hopkins is throwing a fit right now, but the show served its purpose, Briell found love. I am so thrilled he found that love in you, Maria. JaBriell, you better take care of her, because if you hurt her, I'm going to put my hands on you." Angela smiled proudly.

"I promise I won't." He responded touching her belly.

"My little man in there." He beamed with joy.

"How do you know it's a boy? It could be a girl." Maria said looking up at him.

"Whichever it is, I will love he or she, the same way that I love you." Briell assured her.

"I would make the perfect Godmother. I'm just putting it out there." Angela added. The three of them laughed as Squirt and Thadd walked over and hug them both. Maria's team also came over to and congratulate her and Briell.

Once Maria's team and the additional people left, Briell approached Kendra and Jessica to apologize before they headed home. Kendra was cool, but Jessica had no words for him. As she rode off in the Escalade, she shot Briell a bird.

Briell walked back in the villa. The camera guys were packing up their equipment, so they could head out. The chefs prepared a seafood meal for them to enjoy. The meal consisted of snow crab legs, shrimp, mussels, oysters, grilled fish, and scallops. Briell, Maria, Thadd, Squirt, Angela, Teka, and Isabell ate like kings and queens.

After the dinner, everyone shared rounds of drinks, except for Maria. They chilled together for another hour, and Maria whispered in Briell's ear, "I need you to feed the baby. I'm hungry for it right now."

"I love it when you talk nasty." Briell whispered back.

"Good night, y'all. Me and Maria will see you'll in the morning." Briell announced as he stood from his seat.

Thadd and Isabell and Teka followed suit and went into the room. Angela called the cleaning service to the villa. It took them about two hours for them to finish. It was late, and everyone else was doing their thing.

As the cleaning service left, she locked up the villa and said to Squirt, "Come to my room in twenty minutes."

"Why do I have to wait that long? Why can't I come now?" Squirt whined.

"You want to make it thirty minutes?" Angela snapped back.

"Ok, I'll take the twenty minutes." He conceded.

"Oh, I know." Angela said as she made her way upstairs. When she arrived upstairs, she lit some candles and hopped in the shower. When she got out the shower, she put on some sexy lingerie. She cued *Beyonce's "Dance for You"* on the Beats speaker that sat on her dresser. Like clockwork, Squirt walked in the room. She instructed him to sit in the chair in front of her. When the song began to play, she slowly took off the robe and gave him a show.

"Thank you, Lord." Squirt said as he looked at her sexy body in motion. After the dance the two of them made love all night.

When morning came, Angela awoke to her phone ringing. She checked the caller I.D. to see who it was. She wasn't at all surprised to see it was her boss, Mr. Hopkins. She figured her and Maria were both fired after last night's show. "Hello. Good morning, Mr. Hopkins." Angela greeted calmly.

Made in United States
Orlando, FL
04 July 2023

34754598R00114